THE CALL FOR FINIS:

LUST

A.J. TORRES

The Call for Finis: Lust

Cover Art by Hillary Bardin

Content Warning/Trigger

Out of respect for my more sensitive readers, please be advised that this book contains the following: Adult Content, Adult Language, Violence, Death/Corpses, and Graphic Scenes that some may find unsuitable/disturbing.

I dedicate this book to those fighting to show that LGBTQIA+ people exist. No matter what, you are seen and loved, and deserve the right to just be yourself. Don't let anyone tell you otherwise.

OTHER STORIES
BY A.J. TORRES

THE CALL FOR FINIS SERIES
PRIDE
LUST
GLUTTONY (COMING SOON)

STANDALONE STORIES
REVENGE AND FORGIVENESS

CONTENTS

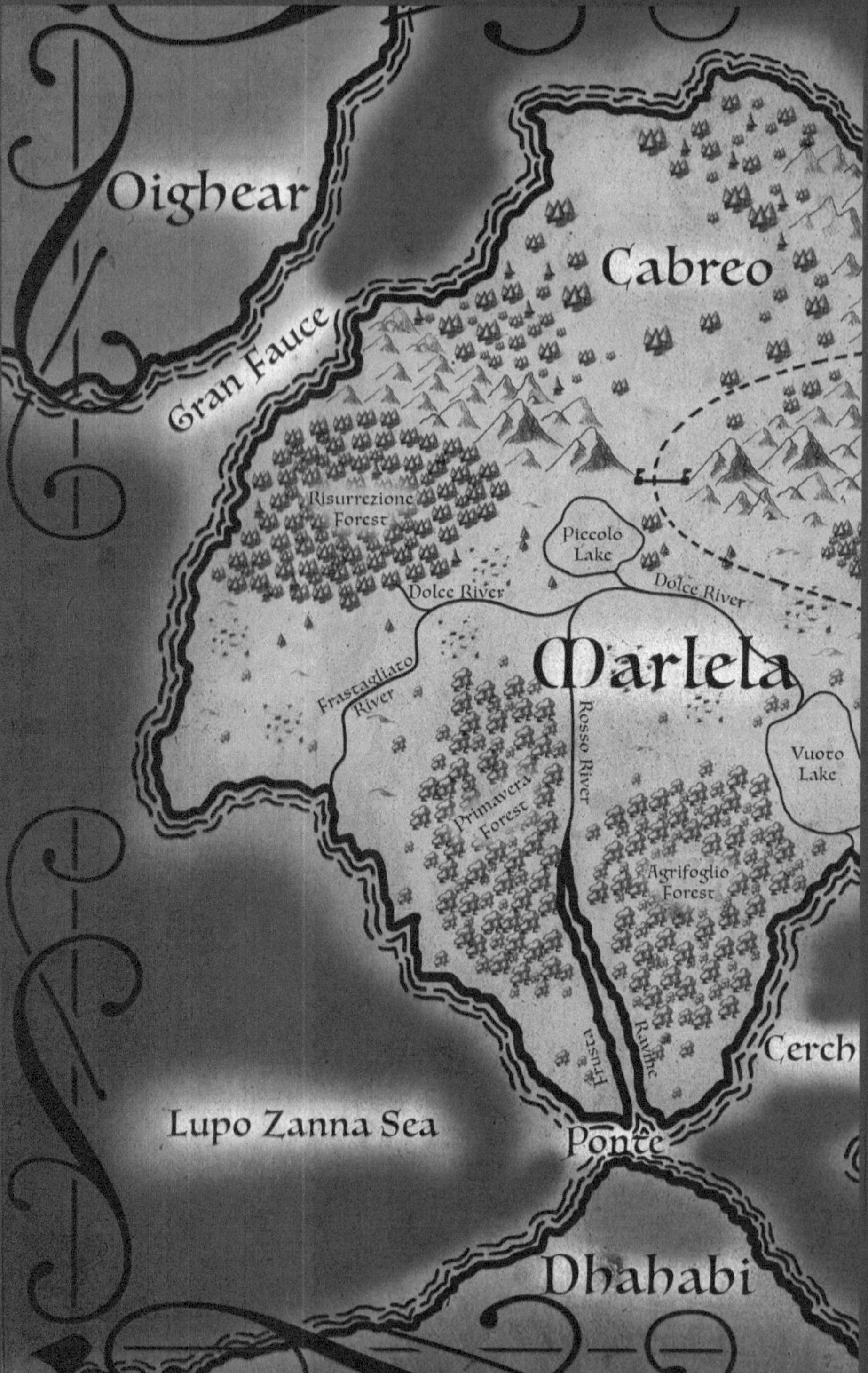
Oighear
Cabreo
Gran Fauce
Risurrezione Forest
Piccolo Lake
Dolce River
Dolce River
Marlela
Frastagliato River
Rosso River
Vuoto Lake
Primavera Forest
Agrifoglio Forest
Frusca
Ravine
Cerch
Lupo Zanna Sea
Ponte
Dhahabi

Marazul Ocean

Utemmet

Marineros

Fiore Pro River

Ringiovanire Lake

Buio Forest

Salvia's Path

Lungo River

Dissolvenza Valley

Virtu River

Luminosa Valley

Lumen Magnum

Rocco River

io Gulf

Aldila Ocean

Dispessore Forest

World of Eldara

THE HOST

FIRELIGHTS DIMLY FLICKER INSIDE LANTERNS, chasing back the encroaching darkness of night. The salty scent of ocean waves mingled with the putrid stench of the recently deceased. A large wooden cart creaked as the wheels sank and stuck in the sand underneath the Lumen Magnum harbor. Two men struggled onward toward the waters.

"Dammit, I can barely see the water," one of the men exclaimed.

"Shut it! Do you wanna get caught? Come on, let's get this over with."

Both men hung their lanterns on the cart and grabbed hold of a linen wrapped body. They pulled it out and tossed it to the sand, landing with a soft thud.

Tsk! How dare they treat him so. A feminine voice whispered angrily from within the confines of her host's shadow. Though the elf's reawakening was a certainty, life had only just started to return to him and so the portal between worlds was at this point no more than a crack. Safeguards would need to be put in place should the host's second chance at life be threatened. As the two men turned back to the cart, a tiny spider birthed into existence from the depths of the wrapped body's shadow. Another body landed on the sand with a soft thud. The arachnid wriggled and stretched its limbs, taking a moment to acclimate itself to the mortal realm, and shifted its body left and right. *Go on, my child, we haven't much time.*

The spider took a few steps toward the body, then quickly scurried onward. Another body thumped to the sand as the spider climbed the folds of the cloth. Searching for an opening, the spider found a small tear in the cloth covering the corpse's face and crawled inside. Claws skittered over soft cloth as the spider squeezed its way between the wraps, until finally touching skin. It made its way across the body's still face, up to the ear, and entered.

Careful my little one. Latch on to his optic nerve without damaging it.

The little spider trod cautiously along the body's cold insides, mindful not to push anything out of place or puncture the soft tissue. As the last body flopped to the ground, the tiny spider reached the eye and wrapped its eight legs around it. The claws latched to the whites and its fangs sunk into the optic nerve.

Now my dear vessel, open your eyes, it's time to wake. I cannot act without confirming they've sinned.

The corpse's eyes opened to a faint gray blur obstructing his vision. A loud gasp escaped his bandaged mouth, startling the two men as they reached down to grab him.

"What the fuck!? I thought these elves were dead!"

"Oi, keep your voice down." The other hissed, shooting him a glare.

"Fuck you! Is he still alive?"

"How should I know? Give me your knife." He knelt beside the body and pulled open the cloth, revealing a youthful, olive-skinned face. His dark brown hair just barely protruded from beneath the wrap. His throat was split wide, surrounded by crusted blood and bruising. Both men stared down at the elf, his green eyes, wide and unmoving, stared into the night sky above. Thanks to the little spider who now served as a conduit for the mysterious voice, she could see through her host's eye. The bodies of the two men began to glow with the color of their sins.

Gray. Sloth is so unpalatable.

The two men stared trembling and wide eyed at the body. Soon, the kneeling man released a soft sigh. "There, see? Nothin' wrong here, just a dead elf— heathenous shit. Now give me your knife." He reached a hand out to the other man, waiting for the blade.

"Why?" The standing man drew his dagger and handed it to the one kneeling.

"To make sure, what else?" He raised the dagger high, ready to plunge the blade into the elf's chest.

No! You must breathe. BREATHE!

The elf sucked in a deep breath, wheezing as his lungs stretched with life, his body slowly reanimating. The wound on his neck began to heal, the skin weaving back together, leaving only a thin faint scar over his olive skin. The kneeling man jolted, nearly dropping the blade, and fell back onto the sand.

"What the—"

"*Oh my, this just will not do.*" A feminine voice bemoaned from the shadows.

The two men turned, scanning, eyes darting left and right as they searched for the source of the voice. Sweat slid down the men's brows. The man with the knife held it forward, his grip tight and jaw clenched. The other man stood completely still as if frozen in place, save for the shaking of his knees. Valdina watched with anticipation as life returned to her host, and thus her pathway into the human world opened. Terror grew in the two men's hearts, and as their fear crescendoed, two pairs of blue eyes, one set just inches above the other, fluoresced from within the vessel's shadow.

"*You tried to kill my host.*" As the shadowed voice spoke, two spiders the size of horses, her children, answered her summons. "*Sinners of sloth aren't really my thing, so you'll feed my children instead.*"

Her two children leaped through the opening into the mortal realm and wrapped their legs around the men's bodies. Only a quick shriek escaped their lips before the spiders' pincers bored into their necks, cutting short the last sounds either man would make. As her children devoured the men, she stretched her arms out from the elf's shadow and pulled her torso through, feeling the weight of the mortal realm pushing down on her.

Damn this realm's pull! It's stronger than I expected.

Valdina hovered over the elf, her white hair cascading around his head. With labored breath, he gasped as tears flowed down the side of his face. He moaned weakly, sounding like the croak of a toad full of sorrow.

"*Shh. Shh. It's alright, my dear Willka.*" She slid an arm beneath his neck and pulled him tight, cradling him as a mother would a baby. Rocking him gently back and forth as she wiped the tears from his face with her long, stone-like claws. "*We'll make them pay for what they did to you.*"

THE PREPARATION

WILLKA STOOD BEFORE A DARK STONE TUNNEL located deep within Dispessore Forest, a fair distance to the south of the city of Lumen Magnum. His brows furrowed as he recalled the stories his mother would tell him before they were parted, of a forest home where she lived before being stolen as a child. There was no way to know if this was truly the home she spoke of, but of all the forests within the borders of Marlela, it was the closest to the city. If any place had a high probability of being the home she had spoken of, this was it. With no way to know what became of his mother, those stories were all he had left to remember her by. The magical totems of her people had to be here.

A chill shot up his spine. The night air was cold, but thanks to Valdina, he felt the warmth of a summer's day across his skin. She channeled the flames of Infernos, the demon realm, throughout his body to chase away the chill.

He raised a hand to the side of his head above his long, pointed ears, running his palm across the recently sheared, dark brown bristles of his hair. The hair on the rest of his head fell long to his shoulders and was brushed to the side. It felt odd but was somewhat refreshing. This hairstyle originally belonged to another, his now deceased lover. The physical trait they now shared gave Willka some comfort, though he wore it just a little differently, parting it to the opposite side. It felt as if a part of his beloved was still with him in some small way, reminding him of the vengeance he would soon wreak on those responsible for what happened. He struggled to force his nerves to settle and began forward into the tunnel, his bare feet digging lightly into the soft earth with every step.

Coming to terms with the events of his life, death, and reawakening would have been too much to bear were it not for the fury driving him to continue forward. Everything had been taken from him. His last moments seared into his mind forever, haunting his thoughts every time his eyes shut, clawing at the back of his mind. Then there was the fact he had been brought back, the feeling of his wounds closing just as excruciating as when he had received them.

Valdina's very existence horrified him. Her love of punishing the wicked was only matched by the care she showed him while he was recuperating after his awakening, somehow making her all the more terrifying.

On the journey here he had come across a small band of rogues. He had not seen them approach. Their footsteps were quiet and thanks to the clouded night sky, he could only see the short distance in front of him. The men descended quickly and tried to rob him. Finding he had not a single coin to his name, that's when it happened. Willka could see the men's sins as clear as a candlelight in the darkness. As Valdina emerged they tried to flee, but their attempt at escape was in vain. They were dead the moment she saw their sins, but they didn't know it yet. Her wicked laughter rolled across the plains. The strange thing was not that she reveled in her duty as a demon, but that when she returned and found Willka scared, she comforted him as a mother would a frightened child.

Shaking the memory away, Willka rolled his shoulders back and forth. It had been a week or so since his reawakening, but his body didn't yet feel familiar. Willka looked down at his hand, curling his fingers inward and then opening them up, again and again. Valdina had told him that the body he reawakened in was his own, and yet, it didn't feel like it.

It is yours, my dear Willka. Valdina answered in his mind. *Coming back from the dead is not something everyone gets to do. It's unnatural to your kind, a gift only meant for a few. It won't be easy, but you'll eventually grow accustomed to it.* Valdina's words were sweet as they washed through his mind, reminiscent of a clamoring of voices from that of a small child to an elderly woman all speaking in perfect unison. It was usually rather unnerving, but at this moment, it felt somehow oddly tender.

"If you say so."

Shush, my dear, I hear voices ahead.

As Willka drew close to the end of the tunnel, he glimpsed the glow of a huge fire. His heart raced nervously within his chest. Willka cautiously peered around the end of the tunnel to search for a place to hide and spotted a sizable boulder just to the right and scurried to it. Kneeling low, he peeked over the boulder. The chamber was enormous with a dome shaped ceiling. A large campfire blazed brightly at the center while smoke billowed upward and out through a circular opening at the ceiling's peak. Around the flames were nearly two dozen elves kneeling atop colorful intricate tapestries, arguing in another language. Listening, Willka recognized a few words here and there as Elvish, a language he hadn't heard since being separated from his mother. Brought up in slavery, he hadn't been permitted to learn the language of his ancestors. Willka's hands tightened into fists, his knuckles turning white.

Relax, my dear Willka. Valdina's words came as a seductive whisper in his mind, making his spine crawl.

I'll relax when Lumen Magnum is nothing but rubble, he bit back, but instantly regretted doing so as she didn't deserve his ire.

She knowingly giggled in reply. *Once we've retrieved the totems so that you may protect yourself, we'll set off for Lumen Magnum. As we agreed, the Finis will see to the sinners and thus, you will have what you truly need.* Valdina fell quiet for a moment, her cryptic words lingering in Willka's mind before she continued. *Now, to the task at hand. Ten of the elves are chieftains. The ones behind them are their protectors.* Valdina suddenly went quiet, which caused his brows to twitch nervously. After a moment, she broke her silence. *I can translate for you, if you'd like.*

You could translate what they're saying this whole time? Why didn't you do so already!? Willka's teeth ground in frustration.

She replied playfully, *I was just waiting for you to ask my dear.*

He let out a soft groan, his head fell forward to rest against the boulder's cold surface. *Valdina, can you* please *translate what they're saying?*

Of course, my darling. One moment, some of them are quite agitated with a few of the chieftains present.

Willka quickly raised his gaze to the elves, intently listening to Valdina's translation.

You see that large elf at the top of the circle?

Looking to the side of the campfire, he spotted a muscular elf decorated with many feathers about his headdress, neck, and hair.

He and the one beside him are dismissing the others' concerns, arguing they should forget about the enslaved elves currently held in Lumen Magnum, and to abandon those who have been recently captured.

WHAT!? Willka's eyes narrowed with anger. Many of the elves' bodies suddenly shrouded over in hues of various colors, catching him by surprise. He had accidentally triggered Valdina's gift of second sight, an ability that allowed him to see the souls of others who have committed great sin.

They're suggesting strengthening their borders to protect themselves from Lumen Magnum. The large one is glowing brightly in yellow, meaning Greed has overtaken him. I'm guessing he's made a deal with the human city. She sighed, boredom clear on her tone. *He wouldn't be the first to sell his people to make his own life more comfortable.*

Willka's eyebrows twitched in aggravation.

A chief to the far side of the circle stood in outrage. She was somewhat taller than Willka and had an athletic build. The feathered chief, however, dismissively waved her away.

She just accused the feathered muscly one of being deplorable for his willingness to abandon their kin. Many agree with her, but the chief to his side retorted that they simply don't have the means to face off with the likes of Lumen Magnum. Hmph, I suppose I understand their hesitance, but if they play it smart, they have a chance of success. Valdina snickered sinisterly.

"I've had enough of listening to cowards." Willka growled.

The chieftains startled, hearing the unfamiliar voice. They looked warily in

Willka's direction as he stood and stepped out from behind the boulder, careful to remain mostly hidden in the shadows.

"It must be easy for you to sit idly by, here in the safety of your forest while those monsters in Lumen Magnum abuse those elves unfortunate enough to have been caught, hauled off and forgotten. Toyed with. Used. Punished for petty grievances." Able to now see all in attendance, Willka scanned the room and several more began to glow. Two yellows, an orange, a gray, a purple, and two reds. "Killed for sport. Many have never even known what it is to live like you do, instead born into bondage. You turn your heads without even considering what they live with on a daily basis. Those of you comfortable with that, well, today you get what you deserve."

Clear enough for you Valdina? Willka mentally asked.

"*Oh, this suits me just fine.*" She laughed hungrily as worry began to spread through the elven congregation, her laughter echoing in the chamber. Her hands emerged from Willka's shadow and slammed down at either side of his feet. He felt her presence rise and loom behind him. "*The greedy ones are some of my favorites,*" Valdina moaned as the strange chatter of her children surrounded them both.

With a flick of her ebony, stone crusted wrist, her children pounced on the elves. Those lucky enough to be spared in the initial attack went for their weapons but were too slow. The waist-high, deep blue and ebony spiders shot out bundles of sticky webbing, trapping the elves inside. They tried desperately to push their way free, but their efforts were in vain. The spiders dragged the captured elves to the back of the cave. Some of the captives hung from the ceiling while others were piled on the floor. A few disappeared into the darkness, to a different corner of the cave, kicking and screaming all the way.

Willka walked forward to the dancing flames in the pit. He stared down at the large fire before him, watching it sway left and right, his mind traveling to memories of his beloved. They had laid on the floor together beneath a thin blanket, bathed in the warm light of the torch hanging from a wall nearby. His partner's golden blond hair shimmered, the sweat covering his golden-brown skin glistening, and his amber brown eyes twinkled against the firelight. A pang of longing swelled within his chest, thinking of the night they shared his cot for the first time. Anguish washed over him in waves, an unbearable ache spreading throughout his body and down his limbs, causing his body to tremble. A deep frown formed on his face.

A loud thud startled Willka. He glanced up as Valdina's eight ebony legs stabbed into the earth, one after the other, stopping beside him. A dense, black exoskeleton covered her entire lower half and partially spread up her humanoid torso, resembling a corset. It also spread from her hands, up just past her elbows and gradually gave way to the pale, bluish skin covering her shoulders, neck, and face.

Her four, glowing aquamarine eyes blazed with hunger as her children brought the muscular, feathered elf to her. The elf chief tried to fight them off, but the web binding was too much for him.

"*Oh my, he looks so scrumptious.*" She wrapped her clawed, ebony fingers around his thick throat, and lifted him as though he were as light as a flower petal.

Higher and higher he rose as she straightened to her full height, the chieftain's feet dangling just above Willka's head. She licked her azure lips in anticipation. As her mouth opened, two sharp fangs emerged, seemingly growing larger as her maw widened. Her bright blue skin stretched tight.

The elf chief screamed out as he stared wide eyed into the abyss. Terror was clear on every fiber of his being. The yellow hue of his soul shrouding his body, slowly ignited and was enveloped in a fiery storm of crimson and orange.

His heart sank into his chest at the sight. As her mouth stretched with seemingly no end in sight, her fangs sank deep into the chief's skin. Willka looked away, trying to ignore the horrible slurping sounds he was sure he wouldn't soon forget.

Glancing to his left, he counted nine spiders crawling toward him, clutching bags between their chelicerae. Their bodies bounced up and down in excitement. He tilted his head and raised an eyebrow in intrigue. Willka knelt and hovered his hand under one of the bags. Just as he did, the spider dropped it onto his palm, clapping its chelicerae.

Willka placed the bag on the floor, making sure it was visible in the firelight. Opening it, he found many tiny wooden figures within. His heart jumped with triumph at the sight. "This is it, the totems my mother spoke of!"

He jolted as a loud thud sounded behind him. Willka turned and saw the body of the feathered chief lying on the ground before Valdina, now shriveled and gray. A horrified look was frozen on its now darkened face. Willka's stomach churned.

Valdina smeared the blood over her mouth, savoring every moment as she ran her tongue over her now crimson painted lips. "*I love wrath but trust me when I say greed holds a special place in my heart.*" She moaned a satisfied hum and hungrily eyed a group of tied up elves nearby. "*Now, where's the other one?*" Valdina quickly scurried over to the other elves whose souls were awash with sin, piled in a different corner of the cave. Her white hair, both loose strands and braids, fluttered behind her. A few of her children followed.

Willka's eyes glanced down to the body of the elf she had devoured moments before. His thoughts drifted to his beloved, wondering if his once beautiful being now had more in common with the corpse before him. His jaw muscles slowly clenched, vowing that the human slavers would pay for what they did to Willka and his beloved. His eyes blurred as he fought back tears, taking a tight breath. Willka then noticed a bag hanging from the corpse's waist.

He quickly looked away, the carnage bringing back memories of his death, and that of his lover. Taking a moment to calm his nerves, Willka glanced at the spiders before him, their many eyes staring back at him, seeming almost as if they were watching with curiosity.

"Ca-Can one of you bring me his totem bag?"

The spider who handed him the bag lifted its body up, clapped its chelicerae eagerly, and scurried to the body in compliance. The other spiders left their bags by his feet. He thanked them and turned to the fire, dumping the totems onto the earth to examine them.

Each totem's appearance was unique, representing a lost loved one. Sifting through the pile, he eyed the symbols etched into them, some on their bases and others on their backs.

Soon, the spider returned from the shriveled elf with the totem bag held high and placed it at Willka's feet.

A group of bound elves, those free of sin and spared from Valdina's devouring, yelled at him in their language. He glanced at them with squinted eyes, noticing their rising agitation, unsure if their anger was solely due to the havoc he and the demons had wrought or if it was something more.

He looked back to the pile of totems, recalling something his mother once said. These elves see the totems as sacred items, meant to be treated with respect as one would their own family. Dumping them discourteously on the ground likely provoked their increased agitation. Although he felt a little guilt for how he was mistreating the totems, he didn't have time to be tender. Willka renewed his search through the totems, ignoring the elves' vitriol.

Totem after totem, he studied the symbols carved into them, each symbol differed from the last, but none were familiar to him. "Damn, what did Mother say again?"

Revealing another totem's base, this one marked with a triangle embedded within a circle and a diamond at its center. "This looks familiar. Is this the symbol?"

Willka buried his face into a hand, thinking carefully on his mother's words. "The square with a circle within and another square is . . . earth, I think. A diamond with a circle was wind, or maybe it was the triangle whose points pierced the circle . . . Or was that water? Damn."

He returned to the triangle with a diamond within. "If so, that means this one should be fire." Willka gripped the totem resembling a feminine looking elf, picturing a small flame in his mind, and hoping the totem would respond. Then a strange warmth crawled its way through his fingers and up his arm. His heart raced, his hand trembling lightly. "Yes, this is it."

Grabbing one of the empty bags, Willka stuffed every totem with the fire symbol into it, leaving the rest. The other totems as he understood them were powerful in their own rights but fire, destructive and chaotic, would suit his needs. He wouldn't need precision for fire. It would spread and destroy all in its path until there was nothing left to burn. It was the perfect weapon to bring ruin to the city that harmed him. Tying the bag to his worn leather belt, he made his way back to the tunnel. "Time to go."

"Alright, come children, where we're going there will be plenty for you all to devour."

The pitter patter of their many legs filled the tunnel with a soft hum. Making his way through the tunnel, the hum slowly softened as the demons disappeared into his shadow, passing back into the realm of Infernos, leaving only the thump of his footsteps, and the distant cries of the bound elves remaining in the cave.

The smell of oak and damp moss filled his senses as he stepped out of the tunnel. The moonlight struggled to breach the canopy of the trees above. He breathed in the earthy scent of the forest, finding a momentary pleasure in the calm.

"These people should consider themselves lucky. No chains, no leather leashes, and not a stone cell in sight."

Soon, no one will ever have to worry about such woes as you've endured, Valdina responded softly.

Willka flinched at the comment, finding it unsettling that such sincere, heartfelt concern existed within the same being who delighted in devouring sinners. He took a deep breath and exhaled. *With luck, Valdina, we will slip out unnoticed, as easily as we came in. I think I've had enough death for one night.*

The sound of rushed footsteps suddenly drew close from behind. He stopped and looked back into the tunnel. The chieftain who had protested against the feathered elf, appeared with labored breaths. Her braided black hair was disheveled and now hung over one side of her olive-skinned face. Worry shone in her amber brown eyes.

He stared at her, bewildered, wondering just how she was able to break free of the spider's webs.

She must have a finely forged dagger to have broken free, Valdina remarked. *Poor thing was probably working at it since my little ones bound her and the others. I like her.*

Willka glanced down to the elven chief's outstretched arms and saw a fresh set of clothes in her hands, looking similar to her garb. A beige buckskin shawl and moccasins with simple white and blue stitching going across them, white top and beige trousers, a blue sash, and a leather belt.

"Only attacked bad chieftains. Here, take," the woman said in broken Anglicus,[1] the common tongue of the humans and their slaves.

His eyes narrowed, a bit wary of her intention.

She took a step closer. "Take. You like us. Like me. Want to help. Take, please." Her posture softened.

His lips trembled lightly. "But I don't know if I'm even one of you. My mother, she . . . she was taken when she was very young, before I was born. She didn't even remem—"

"Does not matter. You know totems. You us." She pushed the clothes to his chest, forcing him to take them, and gently patted the buckskin shawl.

Willka clutched the bundle of clothes, keeping his eyes fixed on hers, baffled by her insistence. He then glanced down at the clean clothes in his arms and then back at her, wondering just how she came to learn Anglicus. "How—"

"Another time. Here." She slid the strap of her satchel off her shoulder and handed it to him.

---

1   This world's version of English

He tucked the clothes under one arm and accepted the satchel. Looking inside, he found a large buffalo bladder, probably filled with water, a piece of thin meat sticking out of one of several parfleches, and the totems he had left behind. "Wait, I don't—"

"You do. Healing totems will help." She pointed to his dirt ridden feet, looking rather worse for wear. "Other totems for . . . vengeance."

Take her kindness, Willka. The nights are cold, and your feet could use the protection. Valdina encouraged.

He looked at his torn and sullied slave clothes, and his blood burned. Placing the gifts on the ground, he began to disrobe so that he could change into his new clothes. When he glanced up at the elven chief, he saw a small smile break on her face. With a bow of her head, she turned away, allowing him privacy.

Slipping on the clothing, belt, and sash, and next the moccasin boots, he took the straps, and tied them about his shins and ankles so that the fitting was snug. Willka then reached into the bag he had stuffed the fire totems into and took one out. Pointing it down to his slave outfit, he thought long and hard on his mother's words: *Ask the spirits within for aid, and with the right totem in hand, they may answer. Light a fire, heal a scratch, quench your thirst, whatever you need. Just ask.*

He took a deep breath and focused his thoughts on the old clothes—*Burn.*

The wooden totem of what looked to be a wolf glowed faintly orange. A spark flashed and quickly flew out wildly. As the spark touched the tattered fabric, his old clothes burst into flames. The fire danced wildly and consumed the linens. He watched as the last remnant of his time as a slave was burned away. Watching the pile of cloth reduced to ash, he felt the weight of his burdens lessen slightly.

"What's your name?" Willka asked softly.

She was quiet for a moment, watching the clothes burn. "Meztli. Chief of . . . this forest. You?"

"Willka." He stood and dropped the totem back into the small bag. Stuffing it into the satchel with the other totems, he slipped it over his shoulder, and began to walk away.

"Come back."

Hearing this Willka stopped, confused, and looked over his shoulder.

"After task done, come back. I take care of you. Promise." She crossed her hands over her chest and bowed her head.

He stared at her for a long moment. The sentiment touched his heart, but the comforting thought was quickly chased away by the uncertainty of an after. "We'll see."

THE MEMORIES

OH MY. GOOD THING YOU ACCEPTED *those cute little totems. That wind one is especially useful, carrying you about on the breeze. With the rate you've been going we should arrive at Lumen Magnum within a couple of days.* Valdina cooed with a soft giggle.

"I suppose so," Willka responded flatly as he reached into his satchel, feeling for the small linen bag of fire totems.

His buckskin shawl caught in the wind, bunching over the lower half of his face. Aggravated, he grabbed a handful of the garment, and pulled it down, hard. His knuckles lightly brushed over the scar on his neck and Willka shuddered. Hesitantly, he uncurled a finger and pressed it to his olive skin, feeling the small bulge of tissue.

Fingers slid along the scar from end to end, just now realizing how far the blade tore through his throat. He paused briefly at the end of the mark on the side of his neck, remembering those last few moments as his life slipped away. Willka then continued, running his finger across his skin to the back of his neck, and down just a little further to the mark giving him renewed life. The disfigured flesh took the form of a pentagram and served as his connection to Valdina.

The scar, although made through unnatural means, felt the same as the one over his neck. It was soft, save for a few rough patches here and there. As Willka pressed down on the scar, he felt a strange heat radiating from within. It was as if he could feel the fires of Infernos trying to come through.

Five days had passed since his return to life. Five days since signing a pact with a demon to get vengeance for everything that had been taken. Their mission, given by the Almighty One, called for a mortal, a demon, and an angel to come together in unison to summon forth Their power to purge sin itself. The Finis, as Valdina called it. He had yet to fully process it all.

Thinking of when we met, my dear Willka? Valdina asked sweetly.

Willka quickly retracted his hand, flustered. "No. It's nothing." He shifted uncomfortably, the color draining from his face and his heart quickening. Taking a deep breath and pushing the thought from his mind, he grabbed ahold of the first totem that rubbed against his fingers and pulled it out. Aiming it down toward the grass, he took a deep breath and concentrated, asking the totem to bring him warmth from the cool night air.

The totem glowed to life and sent a warm sensation up his arm. As quickly as the sensation entered his arm, it thrust back down through his fingers, and out. Sparks began to build and undulate, taking a shape almost resembling that of a small creature, then quickly dove toward the grass. The flame began to spread from a single point in mirrored motion, forming a circle. Just as the ends met, the small flames burst into a sizable fire.

The fire's warmth offered respite from the cool night air. Willka watched the flames dance, then turned the totem over to inspect it against the firelight. This one was carved into the shape of a fox. The natural color of the wood now looked to be somewhat darkened and splintered, as though it had been kissed by flame.

Trying to remember what his mother said, the totems darken either when the spirit was waning, or was set free. He gripped the totem tightly in his palm and sat. Hugging his knees close before the blaze, he found both comfort and pain in its warmth as memories of his beloved flooded to the forefront of his mind. *I need to watch how often I use these.*

Why would you need to use them? Valdina asked, her curiosity surprising him.

"I'm an elf, Valdina. They're not going to let me through the front gate freely. The Templar Equitems are likely to strike me dead on sight, especially dressed as I am in the cloth of my kin," Willka responded with furrowed brows.

"*True.*" She emerged from somewhere behind him, tilting her long, sharp face lightly with a small smile. Her four glowing blue eyes fell on him. "*But you have us. No need to sully your soul, my dear Willka. Let the hate go before it's too late.*"

His eyes flashed open, rage boiling his blood. "What the FUCK is that supposed to mean!?" Willka wanted nothing more than to see Lumen Magnum as a whole burned to the ground.

"*Remember the words of your Guardian Angel after your awakening—'if by the end your anger turns to wrath, you too will be taken by the Devouring.'*"

"Oh please, like you care," Willka growled. He turned away, a scowl on his face.

The cold touch of Valdina's fingers caught him by surprise as they wrapped around his chin and guided his face back to hers. "Don't—"

"*For some reason you don't understand me, Willka. I do care, very much in fact. My duty as a demon is to punish those who are vile. The wicked and evil. Only a sinner can punish a sinner.*" Her eyes narrowed, giving him a stern look.

Willka shuddered. "Only a . . . Valdina, were you—"

"*Mortal? Yes, all demons were, but the memories of that time are lost to us during our centuries of punishment.*" She released her grip on his chin. "*Once we atone for our sins, we are given freedom to live as denizens of Infernos or, should we choose it, to become punishers ourselves, ridding the mortal realm of sin one soul at a time.*"

He stared at her, his lips trembling. "Do you . . . not go to Hevellum after having recompensed?"

She smiled and then leaned her head to one side, her white hair sliding over her bright blue skin. "*No, of course not. Our souls are spoiled due to centuries of punishment. There's no place for us there, which is why our Lord Lucifer has made Infernos a pleasant place for us to live and to punish as we see fit.*" Valdina's eyes turned hungry, making his stomach churn.

"Wo-Would I be punished for taking vengeance?" Willka averted his gaze, confusion swirling in his mind as his eyes welled with tears. "The Marlelains took my life! They took my mother! They took Ikaika—"

"*Tell me about him.*" Valdina wrapped her arms around him and nuzzled closer.

"What?" Willka was taken aback by her curiosity.

"*Your lover, my silly elf, tell me about him.*" Valdina said sweetly. "*What was his name again? Ikaika?"*

Willka stared at her, bewildered. "Why?"

"Mortals' love can be so sweet, so passionate, and so wholesome. Familial love, romantic love, even the love between friends warms my heart. I always seek out that love when I'm punishing sinners. The guilt of hurting their loved ones is often useful in showing sinners the wrongs of their actions, leading them to recompense faster."

His jaw dropped. "I . . . I don't—"

"Tell me how you two first met?" Her blue eyes twinkled lightly.

"It . . . It wasn't under the best of circumstances. I was part of a group, bought and sent to work at a villa near the port within Lumen Magnum. The Mistress took offense at seeing her slaves draped in rags. It wasn't due to some form of altruism though; she believed our appearance was a reflection on her and ordered Ikaika to have us cleaned up." Willka tried not to smile at the memory of seeing Ikaika for the first time.

"Did Ikaika help clean you up?" Valdina teased.

Willka's cheeks flushed at the insinuation. "Oh come on. He was helping everyone." He buried his face into his arms crossed over his knees.

"Uh huh." She giggled.

"Although . . . he did help me with my duties more so than the others." He smiled softly, staring into the crackling fire. "Cleaning the kitchen, the stables, and the halls I was permitted to enter. He even . . . He even saved me from one of the soldiers who guarded the villa. It was well known that he . . . enjoyed fondling *pretty* male elves."

At a hiss, he glanced Valdina's way. A shudder ran down his spine at the nasty glare in her four eyes.

"People like that, I especially enjoy punishing."

"Let me guess, give them a taste of their own medicine?"

"Something like that." Valdina took a deep breath and softened her expression. *"Anyway, tell me what he looked like, your Ikaika."*

His heart raced. "He was beautiful. Ikaika's skin shone a beautiful golden brown and his eyes were bright amber, like staring into a fire." His expression wavered as he reached into his buckskin shawl and pulled out a little pouch hanging by a thin leather string. His sight blurred as his throat tightened. "When he smiled, a dimple would appear on his left cheek. When nervous, he-he would pull at his hair strands, the ones braided to the side."

Tears fell down his cheeks and his breath hitched in his throat. Willka, looking down at the small pouch in his hand, opened it, and pulled out a small, thin golden braid. "His hair . . . was a beautiful golden blond—" He hugged the braid to his face.

Willka thought of his time with Ikaika, unsure if he would be able to do as Valdina said and let go of his hate, anguish, and sorrow. That was all Lumen Magnum left him when they slit Ikaika's throat, all because of the Mistress's new husband. He had been jealous of her elven slaves and wanted to be rid of them.

Ikaika's blood flowed down his neck and chest. They pushed him to the ground. He lay lifeless as the blood pooled around his body and spread to Willka's knees. As they pressed the dagger to Willka's throat, he vowed to take their lives. All of them. No human would make it out of Lumen Magnum alive.

He wanted to make that dream a reality, but now, confronted with the knowledge that his vengeance would cost him an afterlife with Ikaika, could he really go through with it?

Valdina's hands slid over his shoulders and down his arms, wrapping her arms around him and hugged gently. *"He sounds like he was a wonderful lover."*

"He was, and he was mine!" Willka cried out. "He was going to take me to the beach, to where he believed his tribe lived." His heart swelled with pain, feeling like he was being squeezed from the inside out.

Valdina sat quietly beside him, embracing him, and allowed Willka this time to mourn the loss of his lover and that of his own life. She held him until the morning came. The sun breached the horizon, bringing in a new day.

THE CHAOS

ARRIVING AT THE OUTSKIRTS of the great city of Lumen Magnum, Willka ducked behind a clay house. Home after home, he lurked in the shadows of the narrow alleyways to stay out of sight. He made his way through the town heading toward the closest gate which would lead him inside.

Willka, be mindful of your surroundings. Valdina spoke sweetly into his mind. *Keep to the shadows as you are and step quickly to avoid being seen. As you said, you're an elf. We wouldn't want to be spotted by any patrols just yet.*

Spotting several Templar Equitums, soldiers of the Cirine faith and protectors of the great stone city, he stopped and dropped low. The sun beamed down from the middle of the bright blue sky, glinting off the men's armor. They stood before a merchant's stall, two of the soldiers keeping watch while the others looked to be taking advantage of the power their station afforded them.

He couldn't quite make out their words, but from his experience as a slave, he knew the situation all too well. Willka had seen it often enough. The group's leader was likely extorting the merchant, demanding payment for some perceived slight while the men under his command loomed nearby to inspire fear. The ones on either side watched to make certain no one else would step inside. Should the merchant have a temporary moment of bravery, the soldiers would simply kill him and make up a story about self-defense or some other such lie. Hearing the escalating voices erupt, the two keeping watch turned their attention away from the streets to the commotion unfolding. Spotting the opening, Willka slipped by and hastily continued forward.

The small buildings were spaced closely together, constructed mostly of a mixture of clay and wood, with thatched rooftops. Some looked to be heavily weathered but appeared to be livable enough when compared to most slaves' quarters, while others had fallen into heavy disrepair.

Breaching the mouth of an alley several homes over, he skidded to a stop before the South Gate. The white stone walls stretched high and seemed to continue forever to either side of the gates' opening. He crouched and leaned against a home, keeping out of sight as best he could. The soldiers ahead, adorned in silver armor and blue capes, were lounging about seemingly without a care in the world.

He took a quick whiff of the air, catching traces of a familiar earthy scent. *Are they . . . drinking wine? They're supposed to be keeping watch. Useless fucks, the lot of them!*

Valdina sighed. *Drunk and stupid. That'll probably make it easier to slip by.*

Who said anything about slipping by? Willka narrowed his eyes, inspecting the gate and taking note of the positioning of the soldiers. The portcullis was raised high, the wooden doors left wide. A few carts passed in and out of the city.

Without taking his eyes off the drunk, laughing soldiers, he reached into his satchel and fingered for the fire totems. Finding the small bag, he pulled one out. As Willka carefully aimed the wooden totem toward the men, he felt Valdina's unease build.

Wait! Use me, Willka.

Are you crazy! Willka retorted. *Drunk or not, there are too many of them, even for a demon.*

You forget about my children, darling. Valdina's voice dripped with confidence.

Willka pictured her sinister smirk, shuddering at the image. He stared at the guards with anger burning in his chest. His hand trembled. Willka's aim wavered, confusion and rage swirling inside him.

Besides, Valdina continued, *you said you needed to take care not to use the totems too often. It would be a waste to use them now. Save them as a last resort. Trust in my children and I for now.*

He hesitated, rubbing his thumb across the totem. "Fine! You win," Willka whispered hoarsely as he shoved the totem back into the bag.

Keeping his gaze on the men at the gates, he watched as they laughed and whistled at women passing by. Disgusted, he called forth his second sight. The soldiers' bodies shrouded over in various hues: blue for lust, gray for sloth, purple for pride, and many more. Soon, even auras beyond the gate shone through stone walls.

His brows raised and mouth hung open in shock. "By our gods . . ."

Oh my. Enjoy, my children. Before you is a feast in waiting. Valdina let out a soft chuckle as a swarm of arachnids of all sizes exploded forth from Willka's shadow. The ravenous demonlings hurtled toward the South Gate.

The Templar Equitums barely had a chance to react before they were engulfed. The soldiers closest to the swarm fell within seconds. Those remaining quickly drew their swords as the demon spiders readied to pounce.

An array of webs shot in all directions, covering soldiers, carts, homes, and passersby. Willka watched the pandemonium unfold, his second sight separating the sinners from the innocent.

He jolted as the screaming began. Though his hunger for vengeance delighted in the mayhem, the kind elf he had been in his first life watched in horror. Many caught in the frenzy were bound, dragged, and hung from rooftops and stone walls. Those lucky enough to escape the feeding fled through the city gates.

Spear-like legs and pincers ripped through sinners' flesh. Willka's stomach churned as the demons extinguished the flames of sin, one by one, leaving colorless husks surrounded by pools of crimson in their wake.

When the screaming lessened, he emerged from his hiding spot and peered down the main road. More sinners poured into the roads upon hearing the chaos, spiders leapt to greet them. Some tried to retreat, but most didn't make it as far as their doorways.

Willka's heart raced. The sight of the carnage caused his hands to tremble. He was torn between reveling in their demise and feeling sorry for them. He struggled to push back the guilt rising inside him, telling himself they had no right to garner his sympathy. After everything the city had taken from him, his pain and anger swelled, winning out over his conscience. Why should he feel sorry for the likes of them?

Bells rang out across the city. He quickly turned and looked through the gate.

"I guess I've been found out." Willka took a last quick glance at the chaos around him, hatred swelling in his heart as he thought of Ikaika.

Straightening his spine, he walked through the gate, stepping in small puddles of blood now covering the cobblestone ground.

"Alright Valdina, where am I—"

Willka stopped dead in his tracks as several Templar Equitums were rushing toward him with swords drawn. A few of them glowed with the colors of sin.

Willka, use the totems!

"I thought you said to leave everything to your children!" Willka's hand flew into his satchel, frantically grabbing a fire totem, and pulling one out.

There are too many sinners. My children are indulging, she crooned. *Just use that totem to keep the soldiers at bay.*

A shudder ran up his spine as her presence faded. He felt faint.

The soldiers approached, brandishing white, gleaming blades.

His vision blurred and the world around him darkened. Willka's eyes then flashed wide. He looked around, trembling, trying to regain his bearings, but everything around him was different, a memory brought to life.

"Stop it! What're you doing!? We've done nothing wrong!"

A familiar voice echoed through his mind. He slowly turned around and was shocked, finding himself reliving the moments before his death.

Ikaika knelt on the ground. A silver armored soldier stood behind him with a blade to the elf's throat. The Mistress's new husband, dressed in his luxurious azure garb, stood over him with a terrifying grin.

"You expect me to believe that. No. I know what you elves are used for. Your bodies, that's all you're *good* for. You're too pretty, it's unnatural. So says the Great

One." He paused, smiling a little. "No, you *will* die. Most of you at least. A few will be needed to clean away the blood when we've finished taking out the filth. Those spared will need to be disfigured to remove temptation."

The man in azure let out a dismissive chuckle and grinned. With a flick of his wrist, the soldiers carried out their orders.

The blade pierced Ikaika's throat.

"NO!" Willka cried out, the Templar Equitums of the present now mere feet in front of him. He thrust the totem forward and squeezed it tightly. "Please help me!"

A surge of heat ran up his arm. The totem glowed brightly orange and out exploded cinders forming a whirling tempest of flame and fury, startling both him and the soldiers. He watched in awe at the spectacle. As the fires twirled faster and faster, blades of heat shot out, scorching everything in their path—a figure was just barely visible within the twister.

The soldiers fell back defensively. Willka shielded himself as one of the fiery blades hurtled toward him, but to his surprise, it phased right through him. He looked up as a floating figure emerged from the flames. She was tall and slender, elven, with pointed ears and a body composed entirely of flame.

"What—"

She stared at him with bright yellow eyes.

Willka fell silent, at a loss for words in all her ethereal splendor. His heart swelled with remorse, wishing he had believed his mother's stories about the spirits living inside the totems. Until now, he had thought it unreal, believing instead that the totems were simply magic.

"She was right, you really do live in the totems." A few tears flowed down his cheeks as the memory of his likely now deceased Mother turned to that of Ikaika. "Please," Willka pleaded through the lump in his throat, "help me."

The fiery figure nodded and twirled high into the air. She gracefully turned with an arc and crashed down in the center of the small group of soldiers. The fire spirit exploded in all directions, enveloping everything in flames. Those closest to the blast fell to the cobblestones, writhing and badly burned. Some of the soldiers escaped the blast, shielded by the bodies of their comrades. Those still standing swung their blades at the flames as though expecting the spirit to return and unleash another attack.

His heart suddenly swelled with fury. His plea for help quickly turned into a demand for vengeance. Ordering the spirit to burn them all.

More soldiers were approaching in the distance, rushing to aid their fellow guards fighting against the flickering flames.

He looked to the massive stone city towering above. Square-shaped buildings and blue banners as far as he could see. Angelic statues decorated the city, their weapons pointed down as though ready to strike.

Willka stepped into the burning carnage. A large shadow came over him and the surrounding area suddenly. Startled, he looked up. His eyes grew wide, and his body froze in place.

High above the city was a large, dingy green skinned creature hovering in place. It was long with enormous, webbed wings. Every flap sent a burst of wind through the streets. Six thick legs dangled below its wide, otherworldly girth. He spotted a figure atop its back. "Valdina?"

Sorry I was away so long, my dear, Valdina answered. *Interesting though. It looks like the others are starting to get into position. It's time we made our way to our temple.*

"Others?" Willka exclaimed. "What do you mean, others?"

Oh my sweet, did you really think you were the only one carrying out this task? The Finis requires seven souls such as yourself, each with a demon and guardian angel of their own, acting in unison.

"Seriously? Why didn't you say so before?"

I didn't think the information was pertinent, and Eltenian was more worried about your mental state than anything else after he showed to deliver Hevellum's message to us. Now come, more soldiers are almost upon you.

The massive creature then flew off to the North. Willka trembled as he watched it vanish into the city.

Willka, Valdina sang.

"R-Right, okay, I'm going." Willka looked ahead and saw more Templar Equitums closing in on him. "Do I need to fight my way to the temple myself?"

Yes, but just for a little while longer. Use that totem until my children arri— Oh! I spoke too soon. She giggled wickedly.

Willka stared ahead and gripped the totem tightly. He asked the spirit to help him through gritted teeth. Fire sparked to life and swirled around him. The fiery spirit formed once again. She twirled high in the air and came crashing down between the soldiers, setting some ablaze, and knocking others back.

Spotting an opening in the street, Willka pushed forward into a sprint. Spiders emerged from his shadow once again and followed at his sides and back, a small horde making their way through the burning surroundings. The creatures bound innocents and killed those shrouded in sin who were unlucky enough to get in his way.

The city was a blur around him as he ran. Bells rang out from all directions as though the city itself had given way to pandemonium. Screams of terror filled the streets. The people rushed to-and-fro, some barricading themselves in homes and shops.

Amongst all the chaos, two women dressed in the finest of garments, in hues of lavender and pink, tripped and fell to the cobblestone in front of him. Willka abruptly stopped.

His heart thumped, beating against his ribcage like a drum. His blood boiled. Each had long, curly hair, one brunette and the other blonde. They both stared back at him with wide, terrified bright blue eyes and clutched each other's trembling hands.

Willka quickly glanced about, seeing many sinners burning brightly in the colors of their deeds, and yet to Willka's astonishment, these two women before him had not a shade between them. His mind was a whirlwind of confusion. Why weren't these women glowing? Based on their gowns they were clearly of nobility, and to Willka, nobles were vile. Evil. They were monsters. And he wanted them all dead.

He gripped his totem hard, ignoring the pain of its sharp edge digging into his skin. The heat from the totem rose into his arm. Just as he was about to command the spirit to attack, Valdina plunged into his mind.

Willka! Leave them be.

The women quickly stood and ran away as he hesitated.

He took a few steps forward to give chase. "WHY!?" He exclaimed aloud. "They—"

They did nothing to you. Do not blame them for the actions of another. Let the

Finis enact your vengeance. Every sinner within the city will be swept to Infernos, and I promise you this, my kind will take our time in seeing every one of them suffer. It will be done. Everything will be alright. Her voice was calm and slow but did little to quell his rage.

Anger and confusion wrestled for control. He wanted desperately to take vengeance on them, on every single human in this city. It was they who kidnapped him and his kind from their homes, their villages, their clans. It was because of them that he and others were separated from their loved ones, forced to helplessly watch their kin be slaughtered before their very eyes.

"No," Willka growled.

Willka—

"Just tell me where to go!" Willka hunched forward, his eyes tightly closed. As strong as his desire for revenge was, wishing he could replace the endless sorrow gnawing at his soul with blind fury, somewhere deep inside him Valdina's words struck as true. A few tears streamed down his cheeks. All this city had taught him was fear, hatred, and anger. The few moments of happiness he was able to steal for himself were snatched away, replaced by heartache and death.

Though Valdina was quiet for a moment, Willka felt her presence in his mind.

Alright, she broke her silence. *It's a little further still, but if you follow my instructions and run as fast as you are able, you should arrive at the temple in time with the others.*

"Fine." Willka wiped away the tears and forced himself onward, following Valdina's directions as best he could.

Several blocks down, a few bells rang somewhere to the South and citizens' screams filled the air. He pushed back his curiosity at what could be happening in their direction and continued on. Soon, Willka found himself surrounded by tall old buildings deep within the city. The streets and alleys were narrow. He continued into a tight alleyway between two broken homes.

Countless bells suddenly began ringing out all across the city, he turned around to face the sky, but his view was blocked by the massive stone buildings towering over him. "What's going on?"

Danger is coming! This city is in pure panic. Willka, you must continue, Valdina said in a rushed tone.

"Trust me, you don't have to tell me twice." Willka returned his attention to the tight alleyway and ran further in. As he neared the end, he ran into a group of humans at a small intersection.

He stared at them and they at him. Their eyes were wide with fear and mouths slightly agape. Willka's eyes drifted to the tallest of the group. A Soror Fidei, a woman of the Cirine faith dressed in black and white. A coif and veil framed her face. She carried a child in one arm and held the hand of another beside her. She was trailed by many children clinging to her and one another.

Willka inspected the child in the old woman's arms while maintaining a short distance. The child turned her head to him, looking confused. She had the long, pointed ears of an elf.

THE FORGIVENESS

S LAVE TRADER! Willka screamed out in his mind, though he hesitated a moment. The woman wasn't glowing. Why wasn't she, a member of the Cirine faith, not glowing? No way she of all people could be innocent, and he wasn't going to allow her to take the child.

He gripped the elven totem in his hand tightly, feeling the heat rise in his arm. Willka raised the figure to them, causing the group to startle, and demanded the spirit come forth. An explosion of cinder burst out from the totem, followed by a swirl of flame. The fire spirit formed before him, her fiery hair swirling before her face. She looked at him with glowing yellow eyes, head tilted.

"Kill the woman!" Willka spat out, snarling and glaring at the old Soror Fidei. The woman gasped. A few of the children screamed and whimpered as they huddled around her.

Willka! They aren't sinners—

"NO! You're lying! You expect me to believe that some of these . . . *humans* aren't going to be punished? They're all guilty!" His vision blurred and his throat tight. "After everything they've done . . . what they did to me. What they did to Ikaika!"

He stared, unflinching, at the terrified group. His hatred burned deep within his heart, and he commanded again, "Kill her!"

The fiery spirit didn't budge. Instead, she looked back at him with brows curved, and saddened eyes.

A sudden chill crawled up Willka's spine. A large shadow loomed over him from behind, and the children shrieked in terror, taking refuge behind the old woman. He shuddered as Valdina's sharp tipped fingers ran across his bare shoulders and down his arms, sending gooseflesh about his skin. Her rough, ebony stone hand came into view, sliding along his arm to his wrist.

"What are you—"

She clutched his wrists tight, squeezing just hard enough to jerk him back a bit. "*Let go.*" Her voice was stern and chilling.

"What!? No—"

Valdina pulled him back against her, moving closer. Her lips brushed against his ear. "*Willka, you have to let go of your hate, or it will drag you to Infernos.*"

A few tears fell down Willka's cheeks. His breath slowed. Memories of his mother, the little time they had together, flooded his mind. Willka's thoughts then drifted to Ikaika. The first time they met, his smile, stories of his home, and their first of many nights together. The last memory was of Ikaika staring back at him, a sad smile on his face as the blade plunged into his golden-brown skin.

Willka's eyes closed tight. "I don't care!" Everything was quiet, save for the ringing of what seemed to be hundreds of bells in the distance. "You can't . . . If I knew I would get a second chance at life with Ikaika, I never would have agreed to this. I would be with him in Paradise, or Hevellum, or whatever you call the afterlife!"

"My dear Willka."

The familiar voice by his ear startled him. It was Ikaika's voice, but it couldn't be. Why would Valdina mimic his voice? And painfully, how was she doing this?

A strange feeling overcame Willka. A warm wind blew around him, calming his heart, and slowing his racing thoughts. His lips trembled. "Ikaika, is it really you?"

"It's me, my maka maka'oma'o.[1] Eltenian is with me, channeling my words to you through Valdina."

He jolted at the name given to him by Ikaika for his green eyes. Ikaika only ever spoke in his own elvish dialect when the two were safe, alone, for fear of punishment. The words brought more tears.

"It's cruel, I know. The last thing I wanted to do was leave you alone in this world. Gods know I didn't want to, but . . . please listen to me, my Willka, I don't have much time. You have been given a second chance to live. Not just for you, but for me as well. Not many can claim to have such an opportunity, but you do. Go out and do the things you want to do. Do what we were going to do. Together." Ikaika's voice cracked. "And when the time has come, when you're old and gray," he paused, chuckling sweetly, "I'll be right here waiting for you. Always, my maka maka'oma'o."

The voice went quiet. Tears streamed freely down Willka's face. He stared

---

1   Polynesian for *Green Eyes*

blankly forward, lost in thought.

Floating before him a moment longer, the fire spirit then bowed her head and dismissed herself in a whirl of fire, leaving the world for the time being. A wave of heat washed over him. Falling to his knees, his hands slammed to the cold cobblestone ground, and he wept.

Valdina placed her hands on his shoulders, rubbing them as softly as she could.

Hearing the soft patter of footsteps coming toward him, Willka slowly raised his gaze and saw one of the older children walking to him, dressed in commoner garb, a white underdress, and a dingy brown overdress. He cautiously slid back.

She was now standing before him. Willka stared at the girl, looking over her black hair and fair skin.

The young woman knelt and met his gaze with sadness clear in her brown eyes. Her lips trembled. She placed her hands on the sides of his neck, and touched her forehead to his, shedding a few tears of her own. "I'm . . . I'm so sorry for what this city has taken from you. If I can make up for it, I will, just—" The girl startled and looked at the old woman now resting a hand on one of her shoulders.

"Altina, that's enough."

Altina's brows pushed hard together in confusion. "But Heather—"

Heather shook her head at the girl with a small smile and gently pulled Altina away from Willka and Valdina, asking the girl to tend to the other children for a moment.

Willka let his head fall forward. His dark brown hair draped over half of his face and tears flowed freely, his chest hollow.

"*Heather was it?*" Valdina asked, her voice soft and soothing.

Heather nodded, her body stiff in apprehension.

"You have nothing to fear from me, I just wanted to ask you if you could help him, after the coming event is over?"

"Of course, I promised the messenger of Hevellum to aid their hosts with whatever they needed."

Willka winced. The term messenger of Hevellum caught him off guard. He couldn't understand why they would pick her of all people. He slowly looked up to Heather's face. She looked down with an apologetic frown.

"Listen, if you want justice, turn to the divine. Activate the Finis, and you and your beloved will be avenged." She bowed her head and began to walk back to the children.

A monstrous roar suddenly sounded, shaking the cobblestones beneath their feet and causing everyone to jump.

Overhead a shadow flashed, whatever the creature was it crashed into the tallest, lavishly decorated building nearby. He recognized the building to be that of the Concilium Vaticanum, home to the Papa Regem and head of the Cirine faith. Looking up, Willka saw it thrashing its massive wings and turning stone to rubble with each swing of its enormous, crimson scaled tail. The beast was larger than anything Willka had ever seen. His body trembled. Gooseflesh ran down his arms as the hairs on the back of his neck stood on end. He couldn't pull his gaze from the sheer power and destructive force on display. A pillar of flame shot from the cloud of dust and debris, the flames blanketing the sky.

The children all screamed in terror as a second roar thundered above.

He looked away from the giant reptile destroying a symbol of the Cirine Faith. Willka's gaze landed on Heather. "You have to go!"

"Quickly now, take the children somewhere safe and hide! The event will be activated shortly," Valdina commanded sternly.

"Y-Yes of course, come children, this way!" Heather took the children and continued on the path. Rushing the children through the first door on their right, she turned to Willka with a hopeful gaze. "Good luck." She then hurried after the children, leaving his sight.

Willka trembled in place, overwhelmed by the chaos unfolding all around. He had no idea what the beast was, but its destructive force was nothing to take lightly. Could he really do as Ikaika wanted and turn away from his path of vengeance? Why would Hevellum turn to Heather, a Soror Fidei of all people, for aid? Questions swirled in his mind, but no answers came.

He jolted as Valdina's hands touched his shoulders again. He couldn't bring himself to look at her, wishing for nothing more than to be left alone. *"Are you ready, Willka?"*

Willka kept his lips sealed, thinking long and hard on what to do next. He wanted to see Ikaika again, more than anything else, but if he continued on his path of vengeance, that would never be.

Taking a deep breath, he tried to ignore the pounding in his chest. Exhaling long and steadily, he answered, "I . . . I think I am."

THE DEVOURING

AKING THEIR WAY THROUGH THE MAZE of Lumen Magnum alleyways, Willka grew closer to where the crimson dragon, as Valdina called it, had thrashed against the Concilium Vaticanum. Now it was circling over the city.

Willka turned a corner and found a cylindrical, white marble building. It stood barely half the size of those surrounding it. At the top of the structure were five Seraphim angels, the eight-winged beings of Hevellum, carved from marble. Although the angels were all depicted as male, a stark contrast to the myriad of beings present in his vision the night after his awakening, they were beautifully depicted and elegantly posed, each with a different weapon in hand.

"Is this the Temple of Lust, Valdina?" Willka asked, surprised at how different the structure was compared to the angular buildings he was accustomed to.

Yes. You should be receiving a message right about now.

"What mess—" Pain exploded inside his head, and he fell to his knees, clutching the sides of his skull. He closed his eyes tightly, his face scrunching in agony.

Whispers scratched inside his mind. He didn't know who they belonged to, but didn't care to find out, wishing only for them to stop. They were like hot iron nails hammered into his very being.

Beyond the pain, Willka sensed a presence approaching from behind him. Cold stone grazed his skin as something icy nuzzled up against him.

"*It's alright, my dear, breathe deeply. That's it, like that. Not every host can handle the strain of the intrusive mental links of the Lords of Infernos, but it'll be over soon. You're doing so well, my little Willka.*" Valdina hugged Willka closer and gently stroked his hair.

He released a sudden, gasping breath and opened his eyes, blinking erratically. The pain subsided, as though it had never been there to begin with. Willka's mind spun as several words floated in his head, implanted within. He looked up at the temple before him, not able to spot a doorway, but at the face of the structure was a small silver plate just a few feet above the ground, firmly fastened to the wall. A semi sphere of metal, just larger than his palm, bulged out from the plate's center. On the surface of the sphere was a pentagram etched within two rings. A singular triangle rested between each point of the star, each unique in appearance.

As Valdina released Willka from the embrace, he stood up and walked to the sphere. He placed a hand on it and spoke the words that hung on the tip of his tongue. "Cum haec Foedus, ego autem quod vestra Sicut Enim Vas. Autem patentibus quod ita ut Libidine."[1]

---

1   Latin for *With this Pact, I will be your Vessel. Now open the way to Lust*

He startled and removed his hand from the silver sphere. "That was . . . odd. One moment I didn't even know these words existed, and now it's as though I've always known them." Willka turned to look back at where Valdina knelt low to the ground in ways only a being with half a spider's body could. "You demons can be really scary at times."

"*If you think voices entering your mind are scary, you should meet a demon from the Sloth Ring. Trust me when I say they are never to be taken lightly.*" She raised her body up off the ground, now towering over him with a strange but sweet smile.

The world quaked around him, causing him to stumble. Valdina caught him and pulled him away from the temple. He looked at the face of the building, Willka's eyes widened as the pentagram symbol brimmed to life in a bright, azure glow. Two small streaks of light shot up from the base of the wall like shooting stars, one on either side of the glowing symbol. The lights moved in sync, traveling up the wall and stopping several feet above his head. Then the lights turned toward each other, meeting in the center and forming the shape of a door.

Slowly but surely, a section of the wall slid down revealing an opening into the temple. The doorway slid beneath the small marble step, disappearing and becoming one with the frame.

Willka took a few steps forward, about to enter the temple when Valdina's grip on his shoulders tightened, stopping him from going any further. He turned to look up at her curiously.

"*Let my children enter first.*" Her face was calm, but her words stoked the flames of uncertainty in his heart.

Tilting his head, Willka's dark brown hair slid off his shoulder. "Why? Do you expect to find enemies waiting for us down there?"

"Something like that."

He followed her gaze just past his feet, taken aback to find something he hadn't noticed until now carved on the ground, a circle glowing ever so faintly. Willka squinted, finding it somehow familiar, but was unsure from where he could have seen it.

"It seems the secrets of the humans who claim rule over this city run deep. I noticed a much larger symbol similar to this one at the South Gate entryway. I think it was meant to keep demons out, lesser ones than I anyway." Valdina pushed strands of her white hair behind her shoulder with the flick of her wrist. *"I didn't feel a thing when you passed over it and only learned of it from my children. It seems they were late to join us due to the wretched thing. This one here, however, looks to be a little different. I think it's meant as an alert of some sort. My children should be able to pass right through."*

"Sounds good to me, but while we're up here I won't be able to identify sin. So they will have to be cautious to not kill anyone down there. Wouldn't want your children to suffer holy judgment for killing a non-sinner." Willka stood to the side of the door and leaned on the wall. Looking down he found many eyes glowing from within his shadow on the ground.

"Oh, don't worry, they don't need to kill. They just need to bind whoever is down there nice and tight." Valdina grinned wickedly at the doorway, her face darkening as the shadows deepened. Her eyes shined ever more vibrantly now.

Her children burst from Willka's shadow.

The large spiders swarmed the temple and rushed in through the entryway. A chill ran up Willka's spine as he watched them crowd the doorway, squeezing their way between one another as each one fought to be the first inside. It was as if the depths of their hunger had no end. As if they existed only to feed.

Arachnids at the back of the swarm began exploring the outside of the temple. Finding the statues above, they pounced. Their sharp, bladed legs pierced the marble and destroyed the figures, piece by piece.

Willka jolted as one of the statues came tumbling down, crashing into the ground. "Valdina—"

"*Those statues weren't originally part of the temples.*" She looked at Willka and shrugged. "*It's fine.*"

Willka leaned back onto the wall and crossed his arms over his chest. He stared at the cobblestone ground before him. The events of the day played over and over again in his mind. He took in a deep breath, his heart beating hard against his chest, his thoughts conflicted.

This city took everything from him. He had unleashed flame and fury upon it and would have continued out of sheer spite. Willka wanted the people to hurt, the way they had hurt him. The Finis just wasn't enough, couldn't be enough to sate his thirst for vengeance, to fill the void that consumed his soul. He realized now it would never be enough. Nothing would. The wound inflicted upon him couldn't be mended, not by any action of his own or that of any other. All he knew for certain was that he couldn't continue down his path of vengeance if it meant leading him further away from Ikaika. Willka squeezed his bicep. Would his vengeance really place him on the path to Infernos? Wasn't his rage justified?

"*Willka.*"

He looked up at Valdina.

"*They've all gone inside. It's time.*"

Willka turned to the temple and saw the path was clear. "Oh, sorry, I was lost in thought."

She giggled sweetly as he approached the temple's doorway. "*I know.*"

He stopped at the threshold, listening to the screams faintly echoing up from far below. "Well that does it then. You ready Val—" he paused as he looked back and saw Valdina was no longer behind him.

I'm already with you, Willka. This is the way, trust me. He looked down at his shadow, nodded, and hugged the right wall as he slowly descended down the stairway into the darkness.

After some time walking down the long stairwell, he slipped on a wet substance covering a few of the steps and staggered, catching himself on the wall, growing frustrated at the constant darkness. The screaming had subsided now, leaving him in silence and surrounded by endless black. The only sounds filling the way forward were his soft footsteps and a dull hum from below. The quiet was unnerving. He kept his hand against the stone wall for balance. It felt as smooth as marble. Taking another step his foot landed unevenly on the edge of the next stair, sending him off balance and into the wall once more. "Fuck! Why did no one think to put torchlights in here? I can't see a damn thing."

We are almost at the bottom. Come on now, you can do it. She cheered him on.

He chuckled with heated cheeks. "Oh come now, I'm not a child."

I never said you were, Valdina sang playfully.

A short distance further the floor leveled out. He slid a foot forward cautiously just to be certain and sighed with relief. "Finally." Willka raised his hands in front of him to help feel his way forward, still unable to see in the pitch-black hall.

The chattering of Valdina's children and the hum was clearer, the muffled noises of whoever had been waiting at the bottom. His hand bumped into something solid. The wall cut into the walkway perpendicularly, framing an opening. He ran his hand up, across the top, and down the other side. He flung himself forward. Firelight ignited the torches on either side of him, followed one by one into the distance, revealing a large circular room with a dome ceiling, covered in countless webs.

Spiders were spread throughout the chamber, littered across the floor, walls, and ceiling. Their sizes ranged from about the length of Willka's hand up to that of a small horse. The largest of the spiders dragged human shaped bundles of silky webbing behind them. The figures wriggled and moaned, clearly still alive. Willka looked over the many squirming cocoons in awe and shock. He took a few steps forward then stopped, something on the ceiling drawing his gaze. The webbing at the center of the dome was thick and glowed as though it were covering something illuminated.

Webs glowed brighter, then burst open and flooded the chamber with a blinding light. A being wrapped in large white feathered wings dropped in and hovered high above the floor. The light dimmed back to a soft glow covering the figure. Its wings flapped open revealing an angel, one of the order of Principalities, Willka's guardian angel, Eltenian.

The spiders retreated back and gave the angel a wide berth. The moment had finally come. Willka took a deep breath. "Alright, where do I—"

"Willka, wait." Eltenian floated down in the center of the massive chamber; he took another strong flap of his white wings and flew toward Willka.

He took a few steps back taking in the angel's appearance. Eltenian's blond hair was a waterfall of curls down his back and framed his fair face glowing golden.

A silver circlet rested about his head and a silver scepter hung by his white sash. As the angel's sparkling violet eyes fell upon him, Willka trembled. His heart was racing fast. It had been some time since he first saw his guardian angel, and the sight of Eltenian unsettled him. The angel was ethereal, otherworldly, and breathtakingly beautiful. Willka stared in quiet awe.

Eltenian took a step toward Willka, holding out a necklace.

Reaching out, the silver chain spilled over Willka's palm. Eltenian cupped Willka's hand and raised it for the elf to see. His stomach fluttered.

Willka tilted his head to examine the small silver pendant attached to the chain. An amethyst gemstone decorated its center, surrounded by a ring of knotwork. It dawned on Willka that this pendant had been hanging around Eltenian's neck when they first met after his awakening.

"Eltenian, why are you giving me your pendant?"

The angel was quiet for a while before answering. "As much as Ikaika misses thou, he truly wishes thee to experience all of life's splendors, but should thee be unable to make peace with his absence and thine heart wish to be taken from this realm to be reunited with thy love, use this to call me, and I shall take thy soul to him, Willka."

Releasing a long breath, Willka was taken aback by the gift. "I-I don't know what to say."

"*Oh, well that's a pretty pendant.*"

He startled as Valdina peered over his shoulder, her eyes on the necklace and her long white hair tickling his neck and arm.

"*I think you should keep it, for a while at least,*" Valdina continued, raising her body high. She stretched her arms up with fingers interlocked. Valdina stepped away to greet her children, many of which scurried about with what sounded like excited chatter.

Returning his attention to the silver pendant, Willka laughed, staring at it for a moment. The amethyst gleamed in a mixture of firelight and the angel's soft glow. A warm, happy smile creased his face for the first time since his death. One day he would, but perhaps not today. He took the thin chain and stretched it wide, pulling it around his neck and clasped it together to hang alongside Ikaika's braided hair. "I promise you Ikaika, I will live for the both of us." Willka looked up at Eltenian, seeing the surprise on the angel's face.

Eltenian then nodded once and cupped Willka's cheeks before touching their foreheads together. "Then live thy life as happy and free as thou can, and when thou art ready, I *will* come."

"It's a promise then?"

Eltenian chortled warmly. "Tis." As the angel's hands slid from Willka's skin, he flapped his wings and flew to a side of the chamber.

Willka took a few steps forward and watched as the spiders cleared the floor and spread to the walls. A massive symbol encased in a large triangle was etched onto the marble floor, a mixture of the signs of Hevellum and Infernos. A cross with arms of equal length having wide, arched ends, punctuated by a circle at its center rested beneath a pentagram. A single diamond was placed between each arm of the cross followed by three rays of light. Between the points of the pentagram were triangles, each unique in its own right.

Valdina and Eltenian each stood before a silver sphere lodged in the ground at the two far points of the triangle. The spheres were pristine and shone in the torchlight but bore no markings and were untouched by the webs. Willka looked to his feet and saw he was standing at the third point of the triangle, a silver sphere nestled in the stone there as well.

"So what do we do now?" Willka asked, turning to his demon and angel for guidance.

"We place our hands on the sphere and wait for it to begin." Eltenian answered.

Both Eltenian and Valdina knelt in unison and placed opposing hands on their spheres.

Looking at his hands, Willka was unsure which to place down. With a shrug, he knelt and placed his left hand on his sphere. After a short time he let out a soft sigh, bored and uncertain as to what should be happening. As his mind began to drift, he felt a sharp pain pierce his hand.

He gave out a loud groan. Eltenian grunted as well while Valdina remained quiet. Willka looked down and saw a strange cone protruding through the top of his hand. A shot of adrenaline rushed through his veins and his eyes went wide. The muscles in his hand and arm tightened as he fought back the urge to pull his hand away.

The cone opened, locking his hand in place. He quickly looked to Valdina and his guardian. Both remained still, unflinching, which eased his nerves, sensing that somehow everything would be alright. Looking back to his hand, crimson blood spilled from the wound, unnaturally flowing to either side of the sphere as though guided by a higher force. The flow continued along the etched path on the floor. He didn't know what to make of it.

Willka watched as his blood filled the symbol in his corner to the very brim. Looking to the others, he saw Eltenian's metallic gold blood, and Valdina's deep azure blood, nearly black in the dim light, doing the same. The blood of the three flowed along more of the symbol, snaking along the path and simultaneously meeting at the center. The symbol glowed in a vibrant azure hue. The cross of Hevellum on the ceiling where the angel had entered illuminated as well, but instead a bright yellow.

"*Willka.*"

He looked up at the sound of Valdina's voice, his arm trembling. She raised a hand to her lips, kissed the tips of her fingers, and blew it to him with a warm smile. "*It was wonderful being with you, my dear child. I better not catch you in Infernos.*" She smirked, but with a stern stare.

"Valdina, I've enjoyed traveling with you as well," Willka answered, confused by the hint of sadness in her otherwise honeyed words, "but why does it feel like you're saying goodbye?"

The cones binding their hands closed and vanished into the spheres as quickly as they had arisen, releasing them. Willka raised his hand to his face, seeing now how large the hole at the center of his palm was, and exhaled in surprise. It barely hurt.

The azure glow turned an eerie orange, resembling the glow of fire. A strange portal composed of swirling darkness appeared above the blood-infused symbol. As it opened, a massive shadowy figure slowly emerged. Startled, Willka fell to his backside. His mouth hung agape.

The yellow glow above them intensified, turning bright white. Willka shielded his eyes as best he could, blind in its radiance. He tried to spot Valdina or Eltenian, but to no avail. The world quaked and the glow continued to brighten, so much that even with eyes tightly shut, all he saw was white. The light seemed as if, in that moment, it would envelop the entire world.

THE NEW BEGINNING

ILLKA?

A voice called out. Willka's mind was caught in a fog, his body heavy. He could barely move his limbs and felt the cold stone beneath him. Willka tried to open his eyes, but to no avail.

"Willka, can you hear me?"

The voice came clearer now, however, it was unfamiliar.

He tried to move his mouth, but all he could manage was a groan. His face scrunched and eyelids fluttered as they slowly slid open.

The world was a blur, a mix of black and orange haze, likely the glow of the firelit torches about the chamber. He struggled to move his head. His joints ached. Try as he might, his body lay motionless, still.

"Thank the Almighty One, you're still alive."

He knew that voice. A blurry figure slid into view. He blinked, trying to clear his vision. "I remember you." As his sight returned, he recognized the woman's face. "Heather?" His voice was hoarse.

Heather nodded, her white hair no longer hidden, instead tied to the side and draped over her shoulder. Her veil and coif were gone, but she was still garbed in her black dress, common for Soror Fideis. The leather strap of a satchel crossed her tall, thin frame. "Yes, don't worry, I brought help." She looked past him and waved for someone to come over.

Willka tried again to move his body, or at least lift his head to see who she had signaled to. The strain was too much. It was as if the weight of the world was upon him. His teeth grit as he groaned loudly, the sound reverberating in the dome shaped chamber. Giving in, he let his head fall back to the ground.

Heather jumped toward him. "Willka? Are you alright?" She carefully lifted his head and brushed his dark brown hair away from his face with her long, wrinkly fingers.

"E-Everything hurts." Willka took a deep breath and exhaled steadily, hoping it would ease the pain.

"All right, just bear with it for a moment longer. They're almost here." Heather said as she looked up.

Following her gaze, he was taken aback. Elven slaves were approaching, coming to stand around them. They seemed confused, unsure of what to do.

"Anyone here you recognize, Willka?"

Willka scanned over the many faces before him. Some wore tattered slave clothes, others in clothing similar to the garments he had worn when in the service of a master. He carefully looked each of them over, noting hair and eye colors of various hues, facial features, scars, height, even searching for house insignias pinned to their clothes, but he didn't recognize a single soul save for Heather.

With a heavy, disappointed sigh he shook his head. "No, I don't recognize any of them." The words came with difficulty. His heart sank, having momentarily hoped to be reunited with someone, anyone from his past. He felt his hold on the waking world slipping as though he could pass out at any moment.

"Oh, I'm sorry. I was really hopeful one of them would have been a friend. Well, maybe they can become your friends. Can some of you help him up, please?" Heather turned and smiled warmly at the troubled elves.

The group looked at each other for a moment. Then two of the elves nodded and approached. They knelt beside Willka, and as they reached out, one grabbed hold of his left wrist. Pain surged through his hand and arm. Willka howled and jerked back, causing the elf to startle and let go, falling on his backside. He sat up and looked at Willka apologetically.

"Ow! Why does that . . . Oh." Willka looked at his left hand, now covered in white linen bandages, a bright red splotch at the center of his palm.

"I did what I could with what I had available. We need to get you to a healer, I'm sure they'll know what to do with a wound as severe as that." She looked up to the two elves before Willka. "Go ahead, it's alright. Just be careful with that hand."

The two elves nodded and carefully helped Willka sit up, taking it slow with every movement. They flung his arms over their shoulders and lifted him upright. With a moan, he commanded his legs to move but grimaced, unable to move a muscle. His body hung between the elves.

"Wait." Another elf, a woman with bright blonde hair, skin as white as snow, and wearing a tight, albeit clean masculine servant's garb stepped forward. Willka wondered if the unusual dress was due to a quirk of the elves' previous master or if they simply hadn't seen it worth the cost to properly supply their slaves. She turned on her heels and knelt before Willka. "Place him on my back. I can carry him up."

He winced at the idea but knew it would be worth it if it meant escaping this place. She stood taller and broader than most of the other elves. The two elves holding him nodded in understanding and carefully placed Willka on her back. They wrapped Willka's arms around her neck as she grabbed hold of his thighs under her arms. She then stood herself up. He jolted at the sudden height, but quickly settled, his head resting on her shoulder. She smelled of pine and something else, something flowery. It was nice.

"It's alright, I won't let you fall." She glanced back at him, her face still.

Willka chuckled softly. "I don't doubt that, thank you . . . for helping me." Exhaustion crashed over him in waves. The call to sleep was ready to take him.

As he drifted in and out of consciousness, he got lost in her scent. It reminded him of Ikaika. He also had a fondness for perfumes, though his tastes lied with the sea. He remembered Ikaika loved coconuts. Willka sighed softly to himself. He hoped to try one someday.

"Of course, tiny woodland elf," she answered.

The group of elves chortled softly.

The world darkened and grew quiet. They were moving, Willka knew that much, but his new companions' voices sounded muffled and distant. He wondered if his exhaustive state could be due to the Finis, or maybe, there was something more. Willka immediately called for Valdina with his mind, like he did so many times before. He attempted to move, to look for her, but all he managed was to turn his head, resting his forehead on the elf woman's back.

The only answer he received was silence. Willka could feel in his heart that she was gone, their bond broken. A strange emptiness swelled in his chest. Though their time together was brief, he grew to count her as a dear friend, the only one he had left, and now she too was gone. Willka silently wished Valdina goodbye, sure to miss her dearly. The image of her face lingered in his mind as he lost consciousness.

Feeling himself jostling up and down, he awoke moments later and wondered if they were traveling up the stairway, too tired to know for certain. He inadvertently snuggled against the elven woman, his body exhausted. It sounded like she was saying something, but in his state he couldn't make out the words.

Up and up they went. Willka attempted to tilt his head and slowly opened his eyes to a blurry, dark world. Clouds obscured the moon and stars above, shrouding the night sky in a sheet of darkness.

"Alright, we've made it out. How is he?" Heather asked as she walked up to the elven woman and Willka. She held a torch close to him, bathing him in the fire's warmth.

He winced and rubbed his eyes, blinking to clear his vision. His eyes widened at the sight of what lay before him. The once grand city of Lumen Magnum, with its tall buildings and looming walls, was now nothing more than a ruin, covered in rubble and debris.

A sigh escaped his lips. "So, this is what has become of the place."

Heather nodded. "Mhmm, yes. A city once full of wonder and heartache now brought low by the God they scorned in a single event. One, I hope we never forget. The people that were left behind have decided to leave this place as it is, to serve as an example, I think is how Baldric put it." She smiled, seemingly amused at the thought.

"Who?" Willka asked, raising a brow.

She laughed as she shook her head. "Don't worry about it."

"Oh, um . . . Hey, can you let me down?" Willka asked, feeling the fog of fatigue drift away, his muscles renewed with vigor. "I can't explain it, but I think I'll be able to stand on my own now."

The broad elven woman stared at him, her face perplexed, but slowly lowered herself and released one of his legs, and then the other. As his feet touched the ground, he pushed himself off her. Willka's body trembled but seemed to hold.

He attempted a few steps forward, stumbling a bit here and there. Taking a few steps away from the temple, the ground shook, toppling him. The others tried to keep themselves upright, steadying themselves against what was left of the surrounding buildings walls.

As the shaking ceased, Willka turned to the temple. The entryway was closing. The marble slab beneath the floor slowly slid up, sealing the way in. His brows furrowed as he lifted himself up, staring at the temple. It seemed that was it then. From this point on his path was unknown.

"So, what will you do now, Willka?"

He looked at Heather for a moment, however he remained quiet. Another elf approached him, reaching out a hand to Willka, and he took it. He struggled to stand but managed to regain his bearings. Willka scanned ahead, looking to a path before him, seemingly cleared of debris. "Does this lead to the South Gate?"

"Seems like it." Heather walked the path beside him and held her torch high, lighting the area in a bright orange glow. The group of elves were scattered about, all traveling along the path as well.

Willka stared down at the road for a time, thinking over all he had been through. Taking a deep breath, he broke the quiet. "There's a . . . chieftain in what

Lumen Magnum calls the Dispessore Forest to the South of the city. She said she can help me, keep me safe. Perhaps I can start a life there. I don't know." He raised his right hand to rub the back of his neck and slowly tried to close his bandaged left hand. Each time he moved his fingers, pain shot all the way up to his elbow. He needed to remember to use one of his healing totems when he had the chance, but then his breath caught in his throat. It dawned on Willka that the skin on his neck and back was smooth. He frantically felt around the space between his neck and shoulders for the pentagram scar he had received upon his awakening, but it was gone. Valdina truly was gone.

His breath hitched. He slid his hand to the front of his neck, a mixture of hope and fear bubbling for what he might find. A sigh escaped his lips as his fingers slid over the scar from the healed knife wound. Willka's fingers twitched. He let his hand fall to his side, unsure if it was relief he was feeling for the wound that remained, or regret. It would forever serve as a reminder of the worst day of his life, but it was also a link to his past with Ikaika.

"Everything alright?" Heather asked, looking over at him.

"Yeah, I'm just . . . I don't know." Willka's eyes softened, pondering his next move. He wondered just what he should do now that he was a free elf.

"Well, why not accept this chieftain's aid? Think of it as a new start. The remaining elves, dwarves, and all those who were forced here from elsewhere are leaving first thing in the morning. If you want, you can wait until then to make your decision." She flashed him a warm smile.

The two startled, hearing the patter of rushed footsteps approaching. A figure came around the corner of a ruined wall up ahead. He had a small lantern that jostled to-and-fro as he briskly made his way to them.

Skidding to a halt, he stopped right in front of Heather and struggled to catch his breath. "Heather, is tha—Oh! Sorry, was I interrupting?"

He was a young man, a human, dressed in simple commoner's garb, looking to be no older than Willka. His skin was fair, and he had a thin scar over his lips. His hair was silver and disheveled, eyes of a deep azure that shimmered like sapphires against the firelight. Willka thought he seemed quite handsome, even given his current state.

Heather let out a sigh of relief, placing a hand on her chest. "No Baldric, you just gave us a scare, that's all." She laughed warmly. "Is everything alright?"

Baldric looked around to the group of elves, his surprise giving the impression as though it had not occurred to him just how a group of recently persecuted people would react to a human rushing toward them. Some of the elves looked scared, others stood ready in case of attack.

He quickly took a deep breath and composed himself. "I'm sorry, everyone, and no Heather, not exactly." He stepped close to Heather, close enough so that only she could hear what he had to say.

Little did he know, Willka's hearing had always been more acute than most. He could hear a whisper from a mile away if he wished. Focusing, he listened in on Baldric's words.

"We found a girl, at least eighteen or nineteen years of age in one of the temples. She . . . well, it seems she was killed. I assume they got to her before the ritual, but given the wound on her hand, she found the strength left to activate the Finis. Did you know her?"

Heather raised a hand to her lips to conceal her gasp. "Oh no!" Her eyes turned sad. "I-I . . . There's only one other person besides Salvia, of those chosen, who was around the same age. Please Almighty One, don't let it be her!" Her eyes glossed and reddened.

Baldric took her hand in his. "Listen, I came to tell you we are setting up a funeral pyre to honor her for what she did for us. I told them to wait for my return before preparing the body. I thought you might want to—"

"Yes. Thank you very much, Baldric." She interjected with a croak. "I would very much like to be there to say goodbye."

"Hey Baldric, did you find her yet?" a voice called out. A woman with long braided red hair and commoner clothes similar to Baldric's, came around the same corner he had come from. She stopped as she spotted the group, a lantern in hand, as her eyes found him and Heather. "Well that answers my question then."

"Zinnia dear," Heather greeted, "while Baldric takes me to see the girl, could you escort these elven folk to their tents? They deserve a rest after everything that's happened."

Zinnia nodded. "Of course." She turned to the elves with a forced smile. Many of them looked at her timidly, some hiding behind others. "I understand your wariness to trust a human you don't know, but I could really use a bite to eat. Is everyone ready, what do you say?"

The elves hesitated, looking at each other to see who would answer the woman. They were nervous, even suspicious, rightfully given their history. One then stepped forward. "We're hungry, yes, but we'd like for you to stay in front of us until we reach our tents. Just to be safe."

Zinnia nodded in understanding. "That's fine. Why don't we take this path for a while? It should lead to another that'll take us to the East Gate. Will that be alright?"

The elves all nodded in acceptance and most followed after Zinnia as she headed away from the temple.

Several lingered a moment and turned to Willka, bowing in farewell before rushing on to join the rest of the group. The last to leave was the elf who carried him on her back. She patted his shoulder, jostling him lightly to look up at her. "You take care, little woodland elf. I hope we meet again."

Willka was taken aback as she flashed him a grin and turned to go after the group. He watched as she left, in awe. See each other again?

"Willka?"

He turned his attention back to Heather who was standing at the ready to head off with Baldric. "Will you be alright on your own?"

Taking a long, silent breath, Willka grabbed hold of the strap of his satchel. As he exhaled, he looked around the dark surroundings one last time, soaking everything in. "Yes, I think so."

"Alright then, please be careful." Heather tilted her head in a bow and walked with Baldric toward the corner he had come from.

As the silver haired man touched the ruined wall, Willka took a quick step toward them and called out. "Wait!" The two stopped and turned to him. "It's a new start, right?"

She nodded. "It's a new start." Though her tone was somber she gave him a faint smile.

"Thank you for finding me, and . . . I'm sorry for-for attempting to take your life. I was . . . so full of rage and anguish. I—"

"Willka, it's fine."

"No it isn't." He looked at her with furrowed brows, eyes trembling. "You know it's not. I was wrong."

Heather released a soft sigh. "You're right, it's not fine. I'm not going to lie to you. I was terrified. The children even more so."

He looked away, ashamed. Willka's right hand balled into a tight fist. His left hand trembled. He felt something warm and wet flowing down his fingers. "How . . . How are they doing?"

"They are well. Especially Altina, she's quite worried about you, actually."

Willka's heart sank to his stomach. "Can you . . . Can you tell her that I'm sorry . . . for behaving like such a monster?" Summoning his courage, he looked up and met Heather's gaze, his eyes blurring with tears.

The gloom left her face briefly, a glimmer of light returning to her eyes. "Of course. We all deserve second chances."

He stayed quiet for a moment, and then exhaled with a long sigh. "Thank you. Just one other thing, I don't plan to come back. Too many memories. Please understand."

"Of course, Willka. You should go where you'll be happy. Take care of yourself, alright?"

"I-I . . . Thank you again, but I feel like I should do something. Especially for the elves here. Can you give them a message? Tell them to wait just a little bit longer before leaving? I plan to inform the chieftain about them. She's been wanting to rescue the elves who were enslaved here, and I think she'll send for them."

"That's wonderful news, I'll be sure to pass it on. Is there more?"

Willka shook his head.

"Then, I'm off. I hope you find peace, Willka."

"Before you go," Baldric interjected, walking up to Willka. The man reached out and handed him his lantern.

He stared at it for a moment and then up to the silver haired man.

"There's no sense in Heather and I both having our own firelight. If you're really set on leaving this place, then please take this. There's no moon out tonight."

"O-Oh, thank you." Willka said, accepting the lantern.

Baldric placed a hand over his chest and bowed his head.

Willka didn't know what to do and simply nodded. With that, Baldric and Heather disappeared behind a ruined wall.

He stood there for a while, alone for the first time since his death. Setting the lantern at his feet, he reached into his satchel and pulled from it an earth totem. It was high time he got his wound taken care of. Looking around, he searched for a patch of earth, but there was none to be found. Everything was paved over with stone. Unfortunately, he would have to wait until he was outside of the city. With a grunt, he stuffed the totem back into safe keeping and retrieved the little lantern. He watched the flame dance for a moment, then held it outstretched before him, and walked down the path to the South Gate. Once there, he stood silently and turned back one last time to look over the city that had dictated the path of his life for so long. From here on he would choose the path he would walk. Should he ever see this place again it would be too soon. With that he continued past the rubble of what was once the South Gate, leaving the city behind, forever.

THE FAREWELL

A CHILL BLEW IN THE SOFT BREEZE carrying the scent of the sea. The sound of waves crashed against the nearby shore. Willka stared into the bright blue sky dotted with white clouds and took a deep breath, tasting the salt in the air.

It had been nearly twenty years since he left Lumen Magnum behind. Twenty years since he last saw Ikaika, heard his voice, and now after all this time, he had finally found the strength to say his last farewell to his beloved.

He released a long breath. Leaning over, he patted his doe mount, which was named after his mother, Kantuta, on the side of her neck. Her fiery orange fur brushed softly against his olive skin, soothing his mind momentarily from the task at hand. Willka turned his gaze forward as he and his group reached a small dune of sand covered in tall grass. The beach stretched far to his left and right.

Willka looked to his left, following the shoreline, and stopped. His breath hitched in his throat. His heart quickened nervously. He spotted a few elven tribesmen resting by long fishing boats, busy weaving together funnel-shaped traps of smooth, flexible wood. Willka inspected their faces, debating what he should do next.

He wondered if this was finally the place. They looked at every beach village North of Jach'a Quqanaka getting further and further from Dispessore Forest. If this wasn't the place, just how many more could be left to find? Willka turned to meet voices that sounded beside him.

He turned to Meztli, the chieftain who took him in after activating the Finis on the great stone city, now nothing more than a ruin. She was speaking with her lover, Citlali, a beautiful, strong warrior of the village. Citlali was tall, lean with freckled brown skin. Their dark brown hair was decorated with a few braids, and their eyes shone in a bright blue hue.

Meztli whispered something in elvish. Citlali nodded in understanding and gently kissed Meztli on the cheek, causing her to blush. The warrior then slid from atop their stag. As Citlali walked past him, Willka's hands tightened around the leather reins of his doe.

"Wait!"

Citlali stopped and turned to him with a curious look on their face. Willka's body trembled a little.

"Let . . . Let me greet them," he said, and hopped off his doe.

"You sure?" They asked, looking at him softly.

He stopped beside them, staring at the sands beneath his feet. Raising a hand to his chest, Willka touched a pouch hanging around his neck tucked under his tawny buckskin shawl. "Y-Yeah, I can do this." He raised his eyes to Citlali with conviction.

They looked confidently at him in return and raised a hand to his shoulder. "You'll do great. If you need us, we'll be right here for you."

Willka nodded in thanks, took a deep breath, and walked toward the elves. His footsteps dug deep into the white sands, the waters sliding up and down the shore beside him. It took his breath away. He couldn't believe how beautiful it all was. Willka wondered, and hoped, if this was Ikaika's home. The wind rustled the leaves of the palm trees that had grown not too far from the water. The scent of salt and fruits swirled in the air.

He made his way around a log lodged in the sand and soon reached the fishermen. The one closest to him looked up to meet him with a welcoming smile. Willka looked over the elf's swirling black tattoos, looking as though they were rivers flowing about his golden-brown skin, reminding him of Ikaika's that had decorated one of his arms.

"My tautau familiar to ya?" The elf laughed at Willka, his words spoken in perfect Anglicus[1].

"Sorry," Willka said, his cheeks heating up. "Someone dear to me had something similar. By any chance . . . are you of the Nā Lawai'a Kai tribe?" Willka's grip tightened on his buckskin shawl, hoping he had finally found his destination.

"That depends, who's asking?" The elf replied and raised a suspicious brow.

Taking another deep breath, Willka exhaled. "Willka, just Willka. We've spoken to many tribes living along the shoreline South of here, searching for this tribe. We . . . I was hoping they could help me say farewell." He reached inside his buckskin shawl and revealed the small pouch about his neck. He untied it and

---

1   This world's version of English

pulled out a white folded cloth. Willka held the white cloth close to him, against his heart, then held it out to show the elf.

The elf set down the unfinished trap, stood up from the boat, and walked to Willka with a saddened gaze. "You've found us then. Show me." Willka unwrapped the cloth and revealed Ikaika's golden blond braid. The elf gasped softly. "This elf was a Ho'ala 'Ia Ka La?" The other elven fishermen stopped what they were doing and immediately looked at Willka's hands in awe.

Willka grew flustered. "I-I'm sorry, Ikaika didn't tell me he was—"

The elf chuckled warmly. "No, I doubt he would. Golden haired elves like your friend are revered, treated as though they were touched by the sun goddess herself."

"And . . . do you believe that?" Willka flashed the elf a doubtful smirk, recalling how often Ikaika dismissed stories of their gods.

The elf shook his head with a chortle. "Fuck no. They are nice stories, but that's all they are." He then returned to the braid in Willka's hands, and his brows furrowed. "Did your friend die in the Taking, by any chance?" He glanced up at Willka, his expression now stilled.

Willka tilted his head to the side, confused. "The what?" It then dawned on him that the elf was referring to the Finis. "Oh! Right, I forgot the tribes had been calling the event that. No, he . . . Ikaika died a week or so prior." A pang pierced his heart as his mind soared back to the day they had died. The events of that day still visited him in his nightmares. He quickly shook away the memory.

"Alright." The elf looked down at the braid again, remaining silent, as though lost in thought for a moment. "We should be able to give your friend a send-off. He's sun touched, so the elders will surely want to send him off properly to the afterlife. However, because of everything that happened leading up to that day, we're wary of outsiders, even other elves. I hope you understand."

He nodded, knowing full well there had been elves who sold out their own kin for the sake of living comfortable lives. "I do, don't worry."

"Thank you, just wait here while I speak with the elders. It shouldn't take long."

"Thank you, um . . ."

"Akamu." The elf replied with a small smile, causing Willka's cheeks to heat up immensely.

"Thank you, Akamu."

Akamu bowed to Willka and made his way up a dune to a few thatch-topped huts a little ways away, followed by his other elven kin, leaving Willka standing on the beach.

Willka hugged Ikaika's braid close to his heart as Akamu vanished out of his sight. Willka then released a breath and slumped down onto the log. A trickle of tears rolled down his cheeks, but he quickly wiped them away.

Footsteps sounded in the sand behind him and as he turned to see who it was. He was greeted by Meztli as she sat down beside him, a calm smile on her face. "And you thought it would be bad."

He laughed softly, still nervous. "Yeah, I . . . I don't know. I still can't believe I'm doing this."

She looked at him as she leaned back and supported herself with her arms behind her. "Are you regretting coming here?"

Looking out into the sea, the sun slowly lowered on the horizon, setting the water aglow. Willka was quiet for a long moment, then reached into his buckskin shawl and pulled out Eltenian's silver pendant hanging from his neck. The beautiful jewelry shone in the sunlight, and he let out a sigh.

"Ikaika wanted me to live for the both of us. To do the things we planned to do together. I've now been to both our ancestral homes, traveled the regions of our lands, and even sailed the seas, though I kept getting sick." He paused, both laughing warmly. "I've learned how to hunt with the guidance of our spirits, to use the totems properly, to farm and how to prepare medicinal herbs. Now that I'm here, and soon to say farewell to my beloved, I'm . . . not sure what else there is left to do. What else is there that we, I mean, I can do?"

"Was there nothing else the two of you wanted to do?" Meztli tilted her head questioningly, her shining black hair sliding over her shoulders.

Willka shrugged, letting the pendant fall back down to his chest and raised a hand to his hair. He slid his fingers backward through the strands, feeling how long it had grown since he left Lumen Magnum, now stretching midway down his back. He hadn't realized until now just how much time had passed since the Finis. Perhaps this would be for the best. It was finally time for him to move on. He let go of his hair, allowing his hand to fall to his lap, and cupped the small braid in both hands.

"When he remembered the name of his tribe, we planned to start our life there. That was all we could come up with at the time. We were slaves wishing for freedom, dreaming of things that then seemed impossible. We were caught and killed soon after we started dreaming . . . Now what?"

Meztli looked up at the sky with pursed lips and tapped her chin with her index finger. "Well, now you can do anything. Go be with your beloved or live on to old age. You may even allow yourself someone new by your side."

Willka startled and looked at her in surprise. All she did was look warmly at him in return. He began to twirl the pendant, while his other hand lightly stroked the braid with his thumb. "Do you . . . think I can? Should I? Would he be . . .?"

"Well, this is just me, but if I passed away, leaving Citlali here on their own, I would want them to move on. Find someone to make them happy, to live a long and ridiculously splendid life." The two chuckled for a moment and looked out to the sea. Meztli stretched her legs out over the white sand. "I mean, who knows, if you did choose to find someone again, you might find you have new things to wish for."

The wind blew gently, Willka's hair lightly brushing against his face as he watched the sea slide in and out, rolling atop the sand. "Yeah, so many possibilities, it seems." He raised Ikaika's golden blond braid to his chest next to the pendant and hugged both close to his heart. Willka felt a sudden warmth grow in his heart, sending it aflutter. It was as if Ikaika was embracing him in return. He looked up at the sky, his eyes welling with tears and his lips stretched into a small smile. "Ikaika?"

A loud yet soothing sound chimed far in the distance, as though the sky itself opened up. An itch scratched at the back of his mind, the faint memory of a sound heard by him only once before but couldn't place where or when. He stared out far over the rolling sea, but saw nothing amiss, and yet felt a tight knot form in his stomach.

"What was that?"

He turned to Meztli. "You heard it too?" Willka asked with a tight throat.

She nodded, her brows curved low over her eyes, confusion and worry clear on her face.

He looked back up to the sky with trembling eyes. "I-I'm not sure." He answered while his heart sank into his stomach. Had Hevellum called for another Finis? Did no one learn from the example that was made of Lumen Magnum, or had the Almighty One at long last run out of patience?

Hearing footsteps to his left, Willka turned and saw Akamu returning from over the sand dune with a small group of elder elves in tow. His heart began to flutter, and his eyes fell downward to Ikaika's braid in his hand, rubbing the golden strands with a thumb. A spark of relief swelled in his heart, sure that the elders' presence meant he could finally, after all this time, give his beloved the farewell he deserved.

Taking a deep breath, he savored the salty air, letting the sounds of waves washing against the shore ease his nerves. Willka finally found peace and yet, it seemed there may not be much time left to enjoy it. Whatever was to come next, he choose to embrace it.

ACKNOWLEDGEMENT

Thank you all so much for reading book two in The Call for Finis series. If you've made it this far I would greatly appreciate it if you left a review on Amazon and GoodReads. Reviews help authors get noticed by other readers, especially if there's a good amount of reviews.

Secondly, I would love to thank my alpha reader, aka my husband, and my beta readers: Janine, Jamie, Briana, Rita, and Raven. Without your help TCfFL wouldn't be where it is now. Thank you guys so much for helping me perfect Willka's journey of vengeance and healing. I really like stories about healing and wanted to do this right. I put my poor elf through so much lol. So, thank you again for helping me on this journey.

Thirdly, I have to thank my amazing new cover artist Hillary Bardin. Thank you so much for bringing Willka and Valdina to life, seriously they look amazing in your style. I'm so happy to see an amazing cover from you and I can't wait to work with you again for book three and on.

Lastly, if you guys enjoyed The Call for Finis: Lust and want to read more from me, please follow me on Instagram, Twitter, or my Author Newsletter. You can seek out my author website by finding me on social media. I release a newsletter at least once a month with news, updates, first looks, and more. Again, thank you all so much for giving me and TCfFL a chance. I hope you'll enjoy my other stories too.

~A.J. Torres

TEASER FOR

THE CALL FOR FINIS:

PRIDE

AVAILABLE NOW ON AMAZON

OUR BOND

IRE DANCED AND SWAYED, a dot of light in an otherwise endless canvas of black. The flames were the only thing keeping the darkness and nightmares at bay. The light flickered and waved unsteadily as the void crept ever closer. The gloom loomed inward as if it were sentient, compelled by a gluttonous need to snuff out the resting world. A chill glided across the plains and attacked the little light.

Salvia's breath hitched in her throat.

On any other night, she could at least find comfort in the moon's luminous glow and the stars which peppered the sky, but nature seemed determined to mirror the turmoil raging inside her chest. A dense cloud cover had arrived with the setting sun and choked out all celestial light. Her little fire was her one lifeline.

Her hands went scrambling through dirt and grass, searching for the stick she laid close in case the flames needed sparking back to life. The fire was dwindling, and as it receded the nightmares grew bold and approached. Frantic screams echoed all around. Embers floated wistfully through the copper-tinged air. Blood pooled on the ground. Death was everywhere. Fires engulfed everything. Homes. Boats. The pier. Nothing was safe.

Salvia released a trembling breath. Her brown eyes stung. Her breathing grew ragged and heart raced. Flames engulfed her vision, and then suddenly, there was her fiance, Lorenzo Aguado, running toward her. Just as he reached her, a spear erupted from his chest and slammed into her with a wet crunch.

Breathe. A deep, cacophonous, and reverberating voice entered her mind, causing a shiver to run between her shoulder blades. *Salvia, you have to breathe.*

Salvia hadn't even realized she had stopped. Struggling through the fear, she pleaded with her body to respond. Slowly, she sucked in a breath and exhaled. Again and again. She felt a little better knowing she wasn't alone. The memory of the fall of her village, Marineros, was still fresh in her mind. It had barely been a week since that terrible night.

Salvia VerdaderaFe, the girl who survived.

Her first major tragedy happened when she had just entered womanhood. A terrible plague ravaged her village and took her parents. Many others died as well, but the village pulled through. Years later, the second major tragedy of her life happened. Raiders fell upon her town, pillaging, murdering, and burning everything in sight. The young woman was the only survivor.

The smell of iron and burning flesh lingered in her nostrils. Salvia could even still feel the warmth of Lorenzo's blood on her copper skin. Bile rose up her throat, and a queasy ache formed in the pit of her stomach.

Slide your hand to the right. It isn't far. The voice in her head told her. She followed without question.

Dirt rolled loosely under her palm as the bladed grass brushed her skin. The sensation would have tickled if panic wasn't spiraling in her heart. Something hard slid against her little finger, and a spark of hope blossomed to life. She wrapped her hand around the small, round, wooden object. It was her makeshift poker, and just beside it she found the bundle of sticks she had collected before daylight had vanished. She grabbed a few handfuls of twigs and dry brush, then tossed it all into the fading orange glow of the pit.

Sparks flew erratically as the flames spread across the newly added debris. Salvia poked at the branches to strengthen and spread the weak flames. As the warmth grew with renewed vigor, the kiss of the flames sent a prickle across her skin. She released a sigh of relief. Sitting back on her folded legs, her body straightened and her hands fell limp at her sides. Her terrible memories were finally falling silent again, returning to the recesses of her mind. The crackling of the flames quieted. Both warmth and cold evaded her senses. All sensation faded. She felt nothing; not the aching of loss, not the strain of travel on her muscles, not the dryness choking her throat, not even the scent of pine and cedar from the sparse surrounding trees.

She just felt—nothing.

Her poker slid from her hand and landed with a soft thud. Salvia pulled her legs out from under her and slid her knees into her chest, wrapping her arms around them and hugging herself tight. She sat like that for a long while. Her body tensed at the sound of a light grumble emanating from her stomach. She was hungry. It seemed odd to her that that would be the one feeling to persevere where all others had faded to obscurity. At that moment she wondered if hunger was the most powerful driving force in life. After all, more than anything else, everything needed to eat. Hoping to calm her hunger, she placed a hand on her belly and rubbed it in an attempt to quell its muttering, but her hunger only grew more severe.

Turning her head to the side, Salvia found her satchel beside her and reached inside the opening, removing a small parcel wrapped with thin rice paper.

She dropped her knees into a criss-cross position and placed the parcel on her lap. Loosening the white string around it, Salvia unwrapped the paper. Looking down at the contents inside she let out a soft, disappointed groan. Four thick cuts of salted pork were all she had left.

That wasn't good.

There wasn't much left and there was no way to be certain how much longer her journey south would take. She had no map and no idea where the next town could be. With another fierce roar from her stomach, she ripped away a small piece of the pork, barely the size of a coin, and stuffed it in her mouth. Salvia would have to savor what she could and ration what was left until she made it to wherever the Temple of Pride was meant to be.

A face then slowly emerged from the light of the fire. It was ferocious, with horns and fangs, looking almost skeletal. Its eyes were glowing. They stared intently at her. Salvia met the being's gaze, unflinching and unamused, then took another bite of the meat.

"*Hey! You're gonna share aren't ya?*" Ultor, her demon companion from Infernos, asked while forming his fanged mouth into what seemed to be a playful smirk.

The very first time Salvia had met him, the same moment she had heard his voice trickle into her mind, fear froze her as still as stone. It was the night her village fell. Lorenzo was lying dead, his corpse on top of her as fire roared all around them.

Ultor approached and knelt beside her, brushing a few loose strands of umber hair away from her face with a thin, pointed claw. He had grabbed hold of the shaft of the spear and pulled it free of her and her betrothed. The only sound she could make at the time was a sharp gasp.

She found herself panting, a hand clutching her chest as the fire of the pit in front of her danced against the cold night air. The face in the flames seemed nearly incapable of making an expression, but she somehow always knew what the minor movements in the face were conveying. She could interpret the worry in her demon's gaze. Taking a deep breath, she straightened her body and swallowed.

"I thought demons didn't eat human food." Salvia answered, eliciting a chortle from Ultor.

"*Well, that depends on your definition of* human food." He paused on the last two words. The demon then released a deep, throaty laugh as he glanced at the pork. Watching her quietly for a moment, his expression seemed disappointed, likely since she hadn't reacted to his jest. Her posture relaxed somewhat but she remained quiet. With a sigh, he broke the silence. "*You know what? Never mind, your portions are too small for someone like me anyway.*" The demon stated with a hearty bellow. His image faded as quickly as it had arisen.

Salvia stared intently at what was left of the portion of pork in her lap. She ignored the grumbling of her stomach with all the power of will she could muster, knowing full well she couldn't indulge as much as her body was urging her to do.

A loose, dry strand of braided hair slid into view, lightly obscuring her vision. Using only her left pinky finger she pushed it away from her face. She began to twirl it about her index finger and watched the embers as they rose into the quiet stillness of the night, a melancholy hanging over her.

Her hand drifted absentmindedly to her collar bone, then fell to a spot on the very center of her chest. Salvia's fingers slid in a slow, circular motion across the fabric of her traveling dress, searching for the item she knew she'd find hanging there. A slight burning sensation birthed to life within her ribcage, deepening the frown marring her face. She held back a discomforted groan.

Hey, stop that! If you keep feeling like this . . . it'll only hurt my feelings. The demon chuckled warmly. There was an unusual comfort in his words, and while she appreciated his concern there was little anything or anyone could do to extricate her from her turmoil. All she could do was clutch onto the object beneath the cloth, squeezing Lorenzo's final gift.

A pang of guilt pierced her heart. Although they had been engaged at a young age, an arrangement made by their parents, and had known him for a long while, she was never able to truly love. Not as a spouse is supposed to.

Why was that? The practice of arranged marriages was common and many assured her that love would follow as it had for them, but that hadn't been her experience. Was she broken?

She cared for the young fisherman, and they did many things together. She baked him her famous quesitos. He taught her how to sail and to fish. They shared in each other's company and learned the intricacies of each other's thoughts, hopes, and dreams. But no matter what, her feelings toward him never blossomed beyond friendship. She had never felt that spark of something more. Salvia was sure Lorenzo knew of her feelings, or lack of, though she never vocalized it. Perhaps that was why on the night of El Festival de la Rosa de Oro,[1] a popular festival in her home country of Cabreo celebrating love and enduring life's many obstacles, he

---

1   Spanish for *The Golden Rose Festival*

set up a picnic and gave Salvia his final gift. He told her that it didn't matter how she felt for him, that he was and could remain patient. That spark had found him, for her no less. He loved her and believed one day she would feel the same for him. No matter how long it took. He would wait. Unfortunately, that day would never come. The fall of her village came soon after that night.

Releasing a shaky breath, she broke the quiet and asked, "Ultor, is there something wrong with me?"

The demon snorted, as if Salvia had just asked him the silliest question. *Of course not, my young friend. Being an immortal, I've come to learn many things. See many lives in various ways. There's nothing wrong with you. Nothing broken. You are just you. You are young, Salvia, and still have plenty of time to discover who you are meant to become.*

"Hmm," looking forlornly at the fire before her, she chose a different question to ask him, "por qué me elegiste?"[2] Her last words were in the Cabreoan language, the language of her country.

Shortly after meeting Ultor, she agreed to be his host and to take him south to a temple held in the heart of the mortal realm. There, they would enact something the demons and angels had called the Finis. Before embarking on her journey, her king and his sons helped return her slain people to their great god Calamar in the sea.

Through her connection to Ultor, she understood and could speak Anglicus, the language of the people of Marlela, where within they would find their destination south of Cabreo. So much of her understanding of the world had changed in that short time. It was almost too much to accept. Gods. Demons.

---

2   Spanish for *Why choose me*

Angels. Limbo. All of it was real and yet, much of what was preached across the known world was not entirely right, nor wrong. The reality was somewhere in between, a tangled mess of truths and untruths.

She then realized Ultor had stayed silent. He hadn't even emerged from the fire. That was until she felt a presence appear behind her. She sucked in a startled breath and glanced back. Someone, or something, was emerging from her shadow. The figure opened its deep violet webbed wings wide, revealing somewhat leathery wrinkled patagiums stretching between rough, stone and skeletal fingers. A chill spread over her skin like a blanket of ice, gooseflesh forming all over. The being pressed himself against her back. Long, thin arms wrapped around her. What seemed to be skin was as hard and as rough as stone. Ultor's arms shined in an icy violet hue against the dancing fire before them. His wings closed in around her, stopping just shy of enveloping her completely as to allow the fire's warmth to caress her skin.

Salvia sat frozen in place. Had she not understood the gesture to be comforting, as close to a hug as one could receive from a being of his unique composition, she would've been terrified. Fortunately, she did know him. Her heart warmed at the display. Raising a hand to his forearm, she found he truly was as cold as ice. Despite being a demon of Infernos, a realm only ever described by mortals as being a land of death and fire, full of molten pits of unending, unfathomable torment, his touch hadn't a single modicum of warmth. Clearly there was more to the demon's realm than any among the living could possibly comprehend.

"Do you really want the truth or the sweet comfort of a lie?" Ultor finally answered.

The corners of her lips twitched into a smirk, then responded, her words melodious yet somber in her Cabreoan accent. "You know our pact."

"*Of course I do, but I want to hear you say it.*"

Salvia stared into the fire a little longer and took a deep breath. "We shall never lie, and we shall never hate. Our blades will strike true into the hearts of those who have sinned. We will help all who would ask but only should they be deserving. You are my guardian and I your vessel. Now purge our sins."

They recited the vow in unison, their words weaving into a tapestry of beauty and harmony. Their roles were reversed, but the purity and intent behind the vow would shape the bedrock of new beginnings and, possibly, so powerful as to bring everlasting change to the realm of mortals. For good or for ill, that was yet to be determined.

Both remained silent for a moment after, each trying to outlast the other in holding their stern, quiet gaze. In the end it was Ultor who broke first. They lightly began to chuckle, and soon their chuckles turned to laughter as warmth filled their hearts.

She looked down at the salted pork and ripped off a somewhat large piece, then raised it to him. "Here, pruébalo."[3]

Salvia tilted her head, noticing Ultor's hesitation. After a long moment he raised his clawed hand and pierced the sliver of meat between his index finger and thumb. His hands were large and fingers long and thin. She quickly ripped away a tiny piece for herself and watched Ultor, wondering just what he would do.

In their time together she hadn't once seen him eat. Did demons even eat as mortals do, or did he get all the nourishment he needed from Infernos?

The demon eyed the flesh between his claws, turning it this way and that.

---

3 Spanish for *Try it*

Tilting his skeletal face to one side, his expression seemed a mixture of inquisition and caution. He pulled the salted pork up to where a nose should've been and drew in a long breath. His insides flared with light, then faded as he exhaled. Lowering it to his fanged mouth, he took a mousy bite and went still. His eyes stared into oblivion as Salvia counted the moments drifting by. One. Two. Three. The demon's attention then refocused, and his gaze turned down to her.

She couldn't help but snort, both amused and a little concerned. A smile slid across her face as she met his look. "If you don't want it then I'll eat it myself." She stated as flatly as she could.

"*Ha! Go right ahead. I don't think I could if I wanted to, to be honest. I always wanted to try it, to eat as you humans do. A memory lost to me of my life before. Your kind always looks as though they really enjoy it. Unfortunately, it would seem a sensation forever lost to me. For us, mortals are our food. Humans, dwarves, faes, elves, and so many others. The souls of sinners, and nothing more.*"

"Aaaah, I see."

"*Yes, and to answer your question from a moment ago. There was something within you, something that—*" Ultor suddenly paused, a sneer shading his angular, spiked face.

Salvia cocked her head at him with a raised brow. "Ultor?"

"*We are no longer alone.*" A growl reverberated from his chest, taking her aback.

Ultor slowly stood before her, a full seven feet at his tallest, and turned. She ducked as his long spiked tail soared over her head. His wings spread far before her, shielding her view. Salvia pursed her lips and laid her salted pork on the ground, bending low to peek beneath the webbed wings. She squinted and waited for her vision to adjust to the darkness, her heart jumped in her chest. Several knights in azure garb beneath armor of silver and white were approaching atop horses of varying hues.

There were six in all, and based on the emblem emblazoned on their banners, they were Templar Equitums from the capitol city of Lumen Magnum. These were knights of the infamous Cirine faith. Salvia nearly opened her mouth to inform Ultor of who they were but fell silent as the top of the demon's sharp tail pressed firmly against her lips.

Shhh, Salvia, I can hear your thoughts, remember? Just be still, this will only be a moment. The sound of his voice rang in her mind.

She closed her eyes for just a moment, feeling the faint dizziness which came with the telepathic link. Ultor said she would acclimate to it over time and even though it hadn't even been a week since their pact was enacted, she was ready for the dizziness to be a thing of the past. Opening her eyes and blinking the haze away, Salvia inspected the templars as best she could.

The banners were azure with shining gold borders, bearing the silver symbol of an intricate cross surrounded by four feathered wings. They halted their horses' gallop about fifteen paces away from the demon. At the head of the group was a knight donned in large, rounded shoulder pauldrons. His helm was decorated with four long white feathers poking high above his head. He raised his hand to the faceplate, slid it back, and showed his face.

Salvia's breath hitched in her throat. He was a young man that looked to be about her age of eighteen, if not a tad older. His skin was fair. A scar was visible across his thin lips, stretching from just under his right nostril across to the left side of his jaw. For some reason, she couldn't help but wonder how he had received such a ghastly wound.

The dark azure of the young man's pupils glared at her demon friend intensely. Salvia's heart slowly began to race as the knight reached to his side and drew a white sword from its scabbard. The man quickly pointed it at Ultor. "You, demon! How dare you show yourself in our holy country! By the holy light of the Great One above I shall slay you here and now. You will never again tempt an innocent soul."

A long stretch of quiet followed. Seconds felt like minutes. Eventually it was Ultor who broke the silence with a harsh cackle. His cackle grew into a deep bellow of laughter, sending a terrible chill up Salvia's spine. She shrank away from him a little and stared up at his thin back.

Ultor's arms rose at his sides, displaying the large, jagged armor plates that covered much of his body. Shining black blades suddenly protruded from the ends of the armor on his forearms just above his wrists, stretching further than any sword Salvia had ever beheld. He slowly spread his arms and webbed wings. He had become a wall of death.

Salvia had no idea he had such a weapon concealed within him. Taking a deep breath in the hopes it would help calm her panic, she scanned the knights' faces. Judging by their expressions, her fear didn't compare to the dread her demon had summoned into their hearts. Her small campfire suddenly erupted behind her, growing into a raging flame that towered over her.

"*Sin.*" Ultor whispered hoarsely, pulling her attention back to him. "*I sense a sinner among you.*"

The horses began to whinny, their front hooves skittering in place and trying to back away while the riders fought to keep the creatures in place. Ultor's spiked tail slowly flailed left and right like a lion ready to pounce. He leaned forward with a deep growl in his chest, looking ravenous with hunger.

"*Salvia, which one?*" Ultor asked, startling her.

It was time.

Her body was trembling. In order for Ultor to act, she had to be the one to divine the sinners for him. Were he to strike at an innocent, he would suffer divine punishment, so he offered her a means to do as needed. She stood up and revealed herself from behind Ultor, startling the head knight, and raised her left hand toward them, palm facing the sky.

Taking another deep breath, she gently closed her eyes and felt the warmth spark to life on her hand. It grew hotter and hotter, feeling like a small weight on her palm. Opening her eyes, she found a ring of fire hovering over her hand no larger than the size of her head. She raised it until her arm was level with her gaze and peered through the haze of heat and flames. She searched the distorted image within the fire and there, one of the knights began to glow brightly in a sickly yellow tinge. Recalling what Ultor had taught her the first time she tested the ability, she recognized the putrid hue to be the color of greed. She looked to the others, waiting, expecting more to light up as well but was taken aback by what she saw—nothing. Only one of the bunch was a sinner.

Ultor noticed her pause and glanced at her. "*What's wrong?*"

She gently shook her head. "Nada.[4] I suspected the one who raised his sword to you and perhaps a few others to be guilty, but it's just the one on the far right."

"*Is that so? Very well then.*"

He crouched close to the ground, his large, spiked horns pointing toward

---

4   Spanish for *It's nothing*

the knight whose soul was marked by sin. Without a moment's hesitation Ultor rushed forward, causing Salvia to jolt in place. He moved so fast he became a blur and struck his left arm blade through the sinner's chest before anyone had a chance to react. The horses reared with fright, causing the still terrified knights to tumble from their saddles to the ground below.

Raising the sinner high into the air, his body glowed brightly in tones of red and orange that danced over his being, like fire. He hung still, lifeless, but the glow separated and took on a human form of its own and writhed, kicking and screaming in agony. Salvia's jaw locked, her body turning icy cold with the realization of her demon companion's power.

Ultor opened his fanged mouth wide and took in a deep breath. He began to devour the glow as it wriggled and desperately fought to escape. The knights all stared wide eyed and frozen with fear at the horrific sight taking place before them. It was like nothing Salvia had ever seen and judging from the knights' reactions, they too were unprepared for this fight.

As she stared wide-eyed at Ultor, sweat beaded on her brow, and her pulse raced. She thought she had understood, thought she had prepared herself for what was to come. To see what he called The Devouring. Salvia didn't expect it to be like this. She knew this fate was the sinner's own doing. Justice was being dealt for whatever atrocities the knight had committed. She should've been glad to see him sent to Infernos for punishment, but all she felt in that moment was pity. The horrific wail of his scream was otherworldly, bone chilling, and a thing of nightmares. She could almost feel the agony he must've been going through.

Her eyes traveled to the body that had now slid to the base of Ultor's blade. Crimson blood spilled down his forearm and dripped to the grass, muddying the dirt. Flashes of her burning village rushed into her mind again, her people running, screaming for their lives. Many fled to the docks, trying to reach the boats in the hopes that they could escape into the vast blue ocean that had always welcomed them. Others tried to fight, wielding oars, shovels, pitchforks, anything they could find. Unfortunately, her people were fishermen and farmers, not warriors. When she closed her eyes, she could still see their chests skewered by swords, their blood painting their village. Women screamed over the laughter of evil men as they were carried away. Not even the children had been spared. Many were tossed, screaming into burning homes. Those lucky enough to live were taken, likely doomed to a fate of slavery, or worse.

"NO!" One of the Templars screamed out, jolting Salvia back from her memories.

As the soldiers regained their composure they quickly drew their swords. Salvia dismissed her fire ring, dropping to the ground, and slammed the same hand hard to the dirt. Breathing in deeply once more and closing her eyes, she called for the binding magic Ultor gave her to protect herself should she ever be in need. Warmth brimmed to life beneath her hand and spread outward. A wave of heat brushed against her face. The spell was ready. All she had to do was focus on the soldiers, will the magic to hold them in place long enough for her and Ultor to flee—

"Kill the witch!" The voice of the head knight ordered, startling Salvia from her concentration.

She'd never heard the word witch before. As she opened her eyes, her heart skipped a beat. It felt as if time was slowed. She watched helplessly as a bolt soared toward her. Salvia fell backward, but there was no time, there was no way she could dodge the projectile in time. Panic set in. She was going to die.

On instinct she crossed her arms over her chest, closed her eyes, and prayed to the Almighty One and the sea god Calamar, praying to anyone who was listening to not let this be her end. She hadn't expected anyone to actually be listening and waited for the bolt to find its mark. Suddenly a rush of wind slammed into her from above. She heard a powerful flap of wings followed by a loud clang, as if a hammer had struck an anvil.

Adrenaline pounded through her veins as she opened her eyes. She was taken aback at what she found. Soft white feathers covered her view. Her mouth fell open. Salvia leaned forward, reaching out to the wall of feathers with a hand, and just as a tip of her fingers brushed against the soft, ethereal plumes, a golden glowing hand grasped onto her.

"Dost not."

A soothing voice filled her ears, sounding more splendid than any bird's song carried on a gentle breeze, more calming than the laps of waves at daybreak, and more relaxing than a soft bed after a long day's work. She turned to its source. Spreading his wings just enough to reveal his form to her, an angel of Hevellum met her gaze, face-to-face. His features were sharp and chiseled.

Her face lit up with disbelief, staring into his aqua green eyes. She quickly crossed her arms into an X over her chest and bowed her head low to show her respect for such a beautiful being. He bowed his head in return, his ebony hair sliding over his armored shoulders and partially covering his glowing golden-brown skin. The being then stood to inspect Ultor who was still devouring the sinner and seemed to be savoring every bite.

As the last vestige of the sinner's glow vanished into the demon's maw, Ultor tossed the corpse to the side where it landed with a terrible squishy thud. The noise made Salvia's insides churn. Ultor then turned his attention toward the bowman who had fired her bolt at Salvia. He swatted the other soldiers out of his way, as if they were nothing more than a simple inconvenience. The woman with the crossbow visibly startled.

To Salvia's surprise she didn't retreat, instead aiming her spare weapon with a bolt already loaded, and loosed it. Ultor didn't even flinch as he snatched it from the air mere inches from his skeletal face. Unamused, he dropped the bolt to the ground, then grabbed the crossbowman and raised her high into the air, looking poised to snap her neck.

"Ultor stop!" The angel screamed out. A burst of light cracked across the sky, punctuating his command with authority. The tone of the plea caught Salvia by surprise. There was no condemnation in his call. Urgent as it was, there were clear traces of concern in his voice.

"*This human dared to loose her bolt at Salvia! This one needs to be punished.*" Ultor snarled. Whatever bravery the woman moments ago had was now gone, replaced by understandable fear. Her hands quivered.

Salvia jolted, fearing what punishment might befall her companion should he devour an innocent. "Ultor, por favor,[5] stop!" She pleaded. "The woman only acted out of fear of what you did. She knew not her actions! I promise you, there are no more sinners here."

Ultor continued to glare at the knight within his grasp, seething as he slightly tightened his grip around her body. The woman groaned in pain as the air escaped her. She clawed at his rough skin with her free hand to no avail. He brought his face

---

closer to the knight, reveling in her fearful, wide-eyed stare. Ultor sniffed her once, twice, three times, as if hoping for a trace of something that wasn't there.

"*BAH!*" He scoffed, sounding disappointed. "*Fine.*" Dropping the woman, he walked over to join the lightly armored angel and Salvia, helping her off the ground.

Salvia glanced at the Templars who stared in disbelief at what lay before them. The leader slowly stood, his hand-and-a-half longsword still tightly gripped in his trembling hand. Ultor and the angel turned to the knights, causing many of the soldiers to flinch, but none dared attack after what had nearly befallen the bowman moments before. Suddenly, one of the knight's horses cantered over to them. It was the one that belonged to the now dead soldier.

Just as the creature reached Salvia, she slowly raised her hand and cupped the horse's chin. She pressed her forehead against the stallion and gently scratched along his jawline.

Ultor then turned to the angel with an annoyed sneer. "*What is this, Abimelech? I heard the call for Finis, but the sinner's I've found so far are few at best.*"

So the angelic warrior's name was Abimelech, Salvia thought, brushing the horse's gray fur and trying to act as though she were not eavesdropping on their conversation.

"Thou misunderstand, *demon.*" Abimelech replied with an annoyed scowl of his own. "The call was not to end the mortal world of Eldara, but to end a single city."

The demon's profound brow winced in surprise, curiosity rising. "*Oh, a city? Please explain.*"

Salvia noticed the head soldier flinch. He was gawking at Abimelech, likely trying to understand what he was seeing.

Swallowing, she decided it would be good to finish the spell she had started before one of the knights had nearly ended her life with a bolt. It would be unwise to interrupt the angel and demon's discussion. Besides, binding the templars would likely be the best way to keep them safe from further antagonizing Ultor. Removing her hands from the horse, she slowly turned to the fire to not raise any alarm and sat herself down on folded legs. Planting a hand on the ground, she resummoned the binding circle and froze the soldiers where they were.

"The city has warped the views of the Almighty One above." Abimelech started to explain. "They segregate and discriminate against all who art different, and murder those who dost not follow their self-proclaimed *true* faith."

A small, pleased smile then grew on Ultor's fanged mouth. "*Don't keep me in suspense Archangel, what's the city's name?*"

Abimelech rolled his eyes in disgust and continued. "The capitol city of Marlela, Lumen Magnum. The selfsame place where the seven Temples of Sin and Virtue reside."

C | A.J. TORRES

OUR DESTINATION

FTER THE TEMPLAR EQUITUMS had been bound in place, Abimelech quickly introduced himself to Salvia. He was an Archangel of Hevellum, which was of little surprise to her. He was as magnificent as Ultor was horrific. What she hadn't expected though was that he was, quite literally, her Guardian Angel. He had watched over her since birth, whispering suggestions into her thoughts and subtly guiding the path of her life.

This brought on a subconscious worry in the back of her mind that she had never actually been in control of her destiny. The thought would've, given enough time, festered into an unshakeable anxiety that could've caused her to question her every action. Before the question had even formed into coherent words, almost as if he too glimpsed the seed of doubt taking hold, he confessed that he had only ever interceded a handful of times, owing to her kind and caring soul. It was her natural predilection to help those around her with a warm smile and gentle hand. She should've felt relieved, but somehow the knowledge that he had been there for her and yet hadn't been able to stave off the horrors that befell her village, offered little comfort. Her every emotion, every sense had been dulled since that night. Her every sense, that was, save for fear. Fear was becoming her ever-present companion lingering in the periphery of her mind.

Salvia was sure that Abimelech noticed her stoicism. With everything he had told her, surely she should've reacted in any number of ways, but she didn't. She just quietly listened as she reached for Lorenzo's gift hanging from her neck. Her hand was inexplicably drawn to it, needing to know it was still there, that she hadn't lost it.

The angel then knelt before her and cupped her cheek. His touch was warm and her skin tingled where he had made contact. He tilted her head upward until she found herself looking into his aqua eyes, eyes that seemed so sad and shimmered like gemstones in the firelight. Abimelech flashed her a small smile and began to inspect her.

Positioning her head gently left and then right, up and then down, she assumed he was checking her for signs of injury. Though she felt fine, she kept silent and allowed his inspection. In the quiet moments she sometimes heard sharp, hushed whispers coming from where the silver warriors stood, but Salvia paid them little mind. No doubt they would be dealt with soon enough. Divine loss of memory, or something. It wasn't unheard of. In fact, the idea was relatively common in tales from her childhood and now that she had a demon of Infernos and an angel of Hevellum standing before her, it seemed likely to be real.

"Well, I see nothing abnormal since thine awakening." Abimelech said, brushing her umber hair from her view as he intertwined a few strands between his fingers, most likely examining how dry and straw-like it had become.

In the last town she had come across, Salvia hoped to bathe and sleep in a proper bed, but the people were far from welcoming. In the short time she was there it was clear she was being watched. The people did little to hide the seething hate in their looks. They had already judged her the moment she stepped foot into the town. What it was that had given them their motivation for such open contempt was unknown but the rationale didn't matter. It could've been the color of her skin or her manner of dress, or perhaps a general mistrust of outsiders. The fact was that there was little she could do to change their perception given the short time she had planned to be there. So she grabbed what little food the local butcher was willing to sell to her and quickly left. Ultor objected, promising that he would keep her safe, but she felt it was best to avoid conflict as much as possible. Though she didn't care for how the Marlelains were looking at her, she didn't wish for them to come to harm. Besides, she felt safer out in the woods. At least there it was unlikely that anyone would trouble her.

"Salvia?"

She startled and looked at Abimelech. He was staring at her, and his hands gently grasped her shoulders.

"May I see the wound on thy chest?"

Salvia remained silent and simply nodded. Raising her hands to the dresses collars, she pulled down on the purple and white fabric, revealing two scars which overlapped each other between her breasts. A pentagram scar which looked like a brand left by hot irons, her link to Ultor, covered an oddly sewn scar. It was the scar she received from the point of a spear. That scar had been healed by divine, or rather, demonic magic. Maybe both. She wasn't honestly sure. All that was left of it was a long, thin line where the flesh had reconnected.

Hanging just above the pair of scars was Lorenzo's final gift, a small gold rose hanging by a golden chain. Six red pearls accompanied the pendant, three on either side. Salvia couldn't imagine how much it had cost to have it custom made, but it warmed her heart every time she looked upon it.

Her eyes stung as she wondered if perhaps she should've kept the bracelet she made him. Did she do the right thing by leaving it with him in his final resting place? It was a gold chain with a red ribbon interlaced between the links. It was a simple thing, but he hadn't seen it that way. Lorenzo's face lit up the day she gave it to him. His deep brown, nearly black eyes twinkled with joy. It was a gift to him. For him. She hoped he was able to take it with him in the afterlife, whichever one he found himself to be in.

"Salvia," Abimelech brushed his knuckles softly across her cheek, garnering Salvia's teary-eyed stare, "Lorenzo is safe. In Hevellum, I mean." The words were soft, compassionate. A smile rested on his face. His black hair wafted softly in the breeze, brushing against his glowing golden-brown skin.

The words slowly set in, her mouth twitching with realization. "You-You mean—"

"The flow commenced, and he has passed through." The angel answered. "Thine gift, he holds it to his heart, as thou to thine."

Salvia released a trembling breath, and a tear rolled down her cheek. The uncertainty of what fate had awaited him hit her harder than she had realized. She didn't believe he would go below, to Ultor's realm, he was far too kind for that, but now she had confirmation, she had her answer.

"Gracias."[1] She croaked in Cabreoan, her heart a mixture of happiness that Lorenzo had safely passed on, but also sadness that he was truly gone from Eldara.

Abimelech nodded and returned his attention to her scars. "Now, it is strange that thy mark appeared over the wound. Would that not be problematic?" He asked, the question not for her, but for Ultor.

"I have no control over where the mark appears." Ultor answered with a shrug. *"I was told my mark would appear closest to where the final blow had been struck. I've had no issue coming and going as needed, so don't worry."*

Abimelech nodded in understanding and returned to the scar. Grabbing the fabric of Salvia's dresses from her hands, he lifted it and fixed the collars to cover her once more. "When the task is complete, the Mark of Infernos will dissipate, but the other," his eyes intimately met Salvia's which caused her heart to skip, "will remain. Dost thou understand?"

She then realized she had been sitting there slack-jawed and shut her mouth. Salvia hadn't given a great deal of thought to the scars on her chest. Whether they were permanent or not, it felt insignificant to everything else that had happened and would happen still.

Her mind was elsewhere.

Glancing to the fire swirling brightly beside her, she forced herself to nod. If the scars were something she would have to live with, so be it. Let them be a reminder, or more accurately, a reason to activate the Finis. For Hevellum. For Infernos. For herself and the memory of those who were lost.

Salvia jolted as Abimelech brushed a thumb over her dry, cracked lips. Her skin prickled, buzzing with warmth as it had when he touched her cheek. Energy

---

1   Spanish for *Thank you*

then constricted the muscles in her jaw as it raced from her lips into the muscles surrounding her mouth and dissipated into the rest of her body. The sensation wasn't altogether unpleasant, but the jolt had caught her by surprise. It lingered as she turned her head away, and she felt somewhat renewed. Not exactly well rested but neither was she as haggard as she had been in the still moments before the knights had arrived. If the surge of vitality had been intentional, he didn't show it on his face.

"Thou art dehydrated. Ultor!" Abimelech scolded Ultor.

"*Hey, don't look at me.*" Ultor raised his hands in defense, his gaze remaining locked on the warriors. "*In the last town we passed, the people unsettled Salvia so much that she didn't want to linger there longer than needed.*"

"Ye need to do better." Abimelech said as he stood up and walked around Salvia to speak with Ultor, face-to-face. The height difference between the two caught her by surprise. Abimelech stood no larger than an average human, only slightly taller than her, whereas Ultor towered above every living soul present. "Thou have nary a map, not even enough provisions to journey to Lumen Magnum. AND ye were just attacked. Salvia could have died!" Abimelech chastised.

Ultor's arms were crossed over his chest. He didn't turn to meet Abimelech, keeping his watch on the knights and what looked like an amused smirk on his face. The demon then let out a soft chortle.

"Ultor, art thou listening?" Abimelech asked with furrowed brows.

"*I'm always listening, just not always to those who are speaking. That human is foolish and filled with misguided courage. He thinks you to be a mirage of sorts. A trick of my doing.*" He chuckled to himself, clearly ignoring the rising anger on Abimelech's increasingly reddening face.

"I dost not much care what these foolish humans think. Thou must be more careful with Salvia's wellbeing. If she dies—"

"*I lose my vessel and the call will be for naught. Honestly, I know—*"

"I swear to the Almighty One above ye demons art infuriating to no end!"

"*Uh huh, anyway why didn't you show after she became my vessel? Kind of irresponsible behavior for one such as yourself.*"

Abimelech let out a frustrated groan. A light giggle escaped Salvia's lips. In that moment, the two's arguing brought her back to a time before all the hurts she had suffered. The barriers of her heart and mind subsided. Her old self had emerged, fleeting as the sensation was. She quickly covered her mouth. The two had seemingly never met before this moment, but here they stood, bickering like old friends, just like Lorenzo had with his friends in life.

"Clearly thou art ready to change subjects." Abimelech's voice dripped with exasperation. "Not all of the vessels had yet been chosen. I was forced to wait as thou foolishly took Salvia through a land she has never been to!" Ultor interrupted with an eruption of laughter, which only furthered Abimelech's fuming. "I will not allow thee to endanger the young woman. I hast guarded her since she was but an infant."

"*Yeah, you've done a great job of that so far—*"

Salvia jolted and shot Ultor a stern look. "Ultor, por favor,[2] behave yourself. That was unkind."

She couldn't imagine what it was like for Abimelech to watch the chaos unfold around her in Marineros. True, she didn't know him well, but it seemed to her that if it were possible for him to have prevented the atrocities of that day, he

---

2   Spanish for *Please*

wouldn't have hesitated. There must've been limitations on his ability to affect the mortal world, just as there were on Ultor. Her Archangel's trembling eyes spoke volumes. What Ultor had started to say had clearly hurt Abimelech, she was sure of it.

"Anyway, the last few Papa Regems hast slowly but surely warped the message of the Almighty One above, shepherding the people in a direction of war and enslavement. Elves and dwarves art hunted down. Humans from far off regions of differing faiths art murdered as soon as they enter port. In order to save Eldara from destruction, and with the permission of the Almighty One, we must rid the world of Lumen Magnum and its oppressive sinners. The Seraphim believe this may stave off the coming calamity they bring upon themselves."

"Do you truly believe ridding one city of sinners can save their world?" Ultor asked as he finally looked down to meet Abimelech.

The angel stared up in silence. His aqua gaze glanced down, roving left and right deep in contemplation. The moment was long and quiet between the two. Ultor stared at Abimelech carefully, as if unsure of the angel's conviction in their undertaking.

With a deep breath, Abimelech finally met Ultor's glowing violet eyes and answered. "Ay, I dost believe it will work. Ignorant as they may be, I believe the good of the many outweighs the bad in the few. Without the seeds of corruption, they shall blossom anew."

A smirk creased Ultor's face once again. He winked then bowed to the angel before him. *"Then it shall be done."*

Salvia sat quietly, leaving the two be. She turned her head to the burning pentagram on the ground singeing the grass. The templar's bindings held. Looking back, as though feeling the cold azure stare of their leader upon her, he glared at her furiously. He was distrustful. His stare made her heart quicken nervously. She hoped that after this, she wouldn't see him again.

Turning back to the fire and situating herself comfortably on the ground, she grabbed a piece of salted pork and was about to take a bite when her fingers brushed against something soft to her left. She startled and found the soldier's blue banner lying on the ground next to her. The horse Ultor had called for her was grazing beside them. With that acknowledgement she surmised the banner must've slid off the creature on its approach.

Salvia picked it up, feeling its silky surface as she folded the fabric from end to end. As she did, a symbol peaked through the smattering of dirt that clung to the cloth. It was the symbol of the Cirine order. Brushing away some dirt, she inspected the intricacies of the design.

An elegant, pointed cross sat at the center of its crest. The beams of the cross were of differing lengths each resembling the blade of a sword, the bottom beam being the longest followed by a mid-length beam at its top and a short beam on either side, protruding just above its center. Four thorns jutted from a circular medallion resting at the center of the cross, each thorn nestled at the intersection of the beams. Angelic wings surrounded the cross, two above the middle beams and two below.

She recalled several of the wandering Sacerdotis and Abbatis Commendets who had journeyed to her village within the borders of Cabreo, north of Marlela. Some of them had been kind, helpful even. They visited spreading word of the Cirine faith, letting all know they would be welcomed into the warmth, the holy light of the Great One above. All would be saved if only they confessed their past sins.

Other members of the faith came as well, but were not as pleasant, instead choosing to shame and bully the people into joining. As if telling her people they would be dragged to the depths of Infernos for believing in the gods of their parents, pagan and heathen gods as they called them, would actually sway the people. Salvia remembered glaring at them and her blood boiling in anger for the hateful words they spouted. Her fingers holding the pork tightened just thinking about it.

It seemed the order had two sides to it and its members. Oftentimes they would even have disagreements amongst members of their own order. How could she trust them if they couldn't even trust themselves?

Salvia didn't care to listen to the rantings and ravings of that sort of Sacerdotis or Abbatis Commendet. She preferred the kind ones, found their thoughts and beliefs interesting. Many of them admitted to not having knowledge of her people's gods and even welcomed the education she could provide. She explained that for Cabreoan's there was no distinction between angel and demon. They were simply entities of the divine, each distinct and the reason of their actions unknowable. What would be, would be. Those of whom she explained this to, found it fascinating. Still, they encouraged those within her village who were willing, to try the Cirine faith, to embrace a new perspective on belief since some of her people had received nothing but heartbreak from their current idol, but that was to be expected. They hadn't come here to convert, but to convert others. It was the purpose of their pilgrimage after all.

She considered converting to the Cirine faith for a time. She told her late fiancé Lorenzo about doing so, but he worried their ocean God, Calamar, would drown them if she abandoned her faith. Salvia quickly became disillusioned with faith entirely after the attack on her village. With the death of her fiancé, family, and friends, she wondered, feared, that it was her fault. Was it truly Calamar retaliating in anger simply for her interest in the foreign faith? Or was it the Almighty One being impatient? Who was to say? At that point she wasn't sure if anyone had the answers.

When Ultor came to her, he explained who ruled them all. Her God Calamar, the angels of Hevellum, the demons of Infernos, and the mortals of Eldara. They were all ruled by one being, the great light Themself, the Almighty One. The choices made in life were the actions of oneself, not the divine. Abimelech had further explained that he could only offer suggestions, nudges in the right direction, but he couldn't make her do anything. Which meant, when bad things happened, they happened by a person's actions, not guided by some divine plan. The world was given to mortals, to live as freely as they wished, but if the path they tread led toward the world's destruction, was it only then that the divine would intervene?

Salvia's head started pulsing lightly with pain. It was far too much information to take in all in such a short time.

She was surprised to learn how the faiths were tied together, no one belief true on its own. Each was but a shard of the greater truth. Each branch of faith became distorted over time, changed to fit the needs of the people. The Cirine faith was worse than most, perversely changed in subtle ways over time. It existed now as only a reflection of the true faith, recognizable in its origin but corrupted by those with power and influence.

It was possible the blade-like beams of the cross were meant to be a literal depiction of what the Cirine faith was about. Join their faith, or be cut down. Many of the traveling Sacerdotis had said as much. Why must people spout such things? Perhaps a change was needed to help open everyone to the truth.

"Salvia," Abimelech called, pulling her attention to him, "that banner openly disrespects the Almighty One above. Can thou please toss it into the fire?" A hint of spite bit beneath the soft, melodious sound of his voice, sending a shiver down her spine.

His outrage was written across his face. Salvia didn't think a symbol alone could hold so much power. In Cabreo there wasn't one symbol to represent one's faith in Calamar. They had various symbols to represent him. Each was fashioned with a similar, recognizable base, but every idol was unique in subtle ways. A splash of paint here, an etched sigil there. The item only had significance to the person who made it.

Glancing down at Abimelech's chest, she spotted a symbol on his chest plate. It had a much smaller cross than the templar's. All the beams were equal in length and were slightly arched at the ends with a plain circle resting at its center. A ring lay beneath the cross just slightly shy of its tips, interjecting between the beams with four diamonds placed between them. Surrounding the ring and cross were twelve rays of light, three at each corner.

She wondered if the symbol was meant to show the light of Hevellum shining on all beings equally. Based on everything Ultor and Abimelech had told her thus far, that seemed to be the most likely conclusion and while she could've sought confirmation, at the time it was easier to follow through with her task by having faith that her assumption was correct.

Without question, Salvia nodded and complied, tossing the banner into the fire. Sparks flew wildly as the flames quickly consumed the silk banner.

"How dare you!"

Salvia jumped at the sudden outburst and looked back to the Templar Equitums. Their leader's face brimmed with fury.

"You claim to be an angel of Hevellum, yet you allow this witch to burn—"

"THAT IS ENOUGH!" Abimelech commanded with fiery fury. Many of the soldiers seemed visibly concerned by the angel's outrage but if that sentiment was shared by the commander, he didn't show it. Then, in a quieted tone, Abimelech continued. "I will not be lectured by fools such as ye."

Abimelech's voice demanded silence. The rage in his expression scared Salvia, but she knew he wasn't a threat to her. She stood up and carefully approached the Archangel from behind.

"Thou hast blindly allowed people to guide thee to war, bringing death and misery to the innocent under the pretense of faith! Well, not anymore—"

Salvia couldn't take it anymore. Hearing the fury and sadness in his tone caused a profound sense of dread at her very core. His very words caused her skin to prickle and muscles to tense. The air grew as thick as molasses in her lungs. She felt the weight of the sky on her shoulders. Urgency suddenly stirred her into action. She rushed to Abimelech, pushing through his wings and wrapping her arms around his torso. His soft white feathers tickled. Salvia embraced him as tightly as she could, hoping to bring calm to his rage.

It was clear Abimelech was thrown off by her gesture. He went quiet.

None dared to speak, not even Ultor or the commander of the knights. It was as if everyone had felt what she felt, the weight of divinity raining down on everyone within earshot, pouring forth from his every word. Ultor was mighty in his own right but to anger an angel seemed an entirely different matter. Eventually, she felt a warm palm press against the back of her hands. His silver armor bit coldly under her palms. He finally took a deep breath and as the air exited his body, the sensation plaguing her body subsided.

"Archangel," Ultor called, *"by any chance have you brought something for Salvia? Perhaps a means to buy food for her journey to Lumen Magnum? As you can see, she barely has any left. I sense there is a town not more than a day's ride or so from here. What she has may not last until then. If not, we can take whatever these so-called soldiers have on them. That should last her until we reach our destination."*

Abimelech sighed. "Unfortunately, nay, I did not." He raised his other hand to Salvia's, gently removing them from his chest. His expression softened after no doubt seeing the worry in her brown eyes, but she hoped he didn't notice. She mustered as much warmth and care as she possibly could in her smile.

His lips then slid into a small smirk of his own, and he thanked her. Raising a hand to her head, he ran his fingers gently through her hair as a parent would their child. "But I hast another method. Salvia, please hold out thy hands."

She tilted her head curiously at him but did as he asked and raised her cupped hands before him. He casually reached behind his back while raising his other hand to hover just above hers. Then, in one swift motion, he swung a hidden dagger past his palm.

Salvia winced at the sudden motion and looked at Abimelech's palm. A small gash on his skin slid open and a gold liquid spilled forth.

She gasped, flinching to grab the Archangel's hand to stem the bleeding, but Ultor placed a heavy hand on her shoulder, keeping her in place. *"Be still, Salvia. It's alright."*

Her stomach churned into a tight knot at the sight of the wound, but she did as she was asked. The angel then curled his fingers into fists, squeezing his hand. A drop of his golden blood fell to her palms and landed with more heft than she had expected. As more droplets fell, she was taken aback as the blood slowly wriggled about, forming into multiple small, yet unknown shapes. The liquid began to harden, each drop forming into small, thin golden discs. So many formed that they began spilling out of her hands. Salvia stared on in awe of Abimelech's gift, his blood now solid gold coins in the palms of her hands.

Abimelech sheathed his dagger and opened the palm of his right hand once more. The wound was fully healed. He then gently cupped her hands within his. "Take these to buy all that thou may need on thy journey to the city of these sinners. Thou must be careful from now on. Dost thou understand?"

Salvia looked up at Abimelech, then down to the coins in her hands, in awe of the gift. He had bled for her. He was an angel, a being of great significance second only to the Almighty One, and he had offered his blood freely for her sake. Had she any feelings of apprehension left about her given mission, they were gone. She would see this through for all who had sacrificed leading to this moment. She returned her gaze to him again and nodded in thanks.

Abimelech smiled happily, cupping her face in his hands, and leaned forward to kiss her forehead gently. "I wish thou safe travels."

Ultor raised Salvia's open satchel. She slid the coins into the mouth of the bag and dropped them in. Quickly kneeling to pick up the coins on the ground, Salvia placed them into the bag as well. Grabbing the satchel from Ultor, she closed it and turned to face Abimelech with a gracious bow. She stood straight with a small, thankful smile and returned to sit by the fire.

Salvia then glanced up to Ultor, to ask how they should proceed. As she started to form the question she paused, tilting her head at the smirk growing on his skeletal face.

"*Abimelech, enact Vovete on the Captain and the Crossbow woman. Their skills will be useful.*" Ultor said, his furrowed gaze locked on the soldiers who were visibly unsettled by his expression.

"Excuse me?" Abimelech asked with a raised brow.

"*I may not be able to materialize quickly enough to defend Salvia every time she gets herself into danger. Also, a prolonged battle could prove problematic for just me alone. Our bond should strengthen over time, but as it is now, I haven't much strength left.*"

Salvia had no idea the bond caused such a strain on Ultor. She was about to stand again but felt a sudden weight on her head. Looking up, Ultor's large hand was over her, seemingly knowing how she felt. "*Stop that,*" he said with charm in his voice. "*I didn't mean to imply that you're a burden. Despite my features, I care for you, even if you are annoyingly too trusting.*" He chuckled warmly, causing her to chuckle. Ultor then looked at Abimelech with a stern gaze, waiting for a response.

The Archangel stared at the demon a moment longer, then sighed heavily. "Alright, I will enact Vovete on the two. The other soldiers will have their memories altered of this encounter, and I will order them to return to whence they came."

Salvia felt a pang in her chest. She glanced at the soldiers, at the two Ultor mentioned would be traveling with her. Would they really keep her safe, even by force?

Their looks were glaring. They had judged her the moment they laid eyes on her. Hated her before she had taken a single action against them. And now they would be bound to her. Anxiety slowly rose within her. Being around such people made her nervous. They weren't to be trusted, and most often, couldn't be reasoned with. However, Ultor and Abimelech knew what they were doing. She trusted them. So, Salvia would trust in faith.

About the Author

Adlin(A.J.) Kennedy Torres is a writer who likes to dabble as an anime artist for fun. She enjoys Fantasy and Science Fiction stories. Adlin particularly loves to write Fantasy and easily gets immersed in books like The Goddess of Nothing at All and Aletheia. She's loved Fantasy stories ever since she was a kid picking up The Lord of the Rings and Eragon for the first time.

Nowadays you can find Adlin in the hot and horribly humid sunshine state of Florida, hanging out, playing video games with her husband, and chasing her son around the house with two needy dogs and a very chill cat.

Instagram and Twitter: @A_J_Torres0